Sins of a Duke

a Scandalous House of Calydon novel

Sins of a Duke

a Scandalous House of Calydon novel

STACY REID

Entangled Publishing, LLC
2614 South Timberline Road
Suite 109
Fort Collins, CO 80525
Visit our website at www.entangledpublishing.com.

Scandalous is an imprint of Entangled Publishing, LLC.

Edited by Nina Bruhns and Alycia Tornetta
Cover design by Libby Murphy
Cover art by Dollar Photo Club

ISBN 978-1-50866-492-5

Manufactured in the United States of America

First Edition March 2015

Scandalous
an Entangled imprint

For Dusean. You are too amazing.

Chapter One

Lady Constance Thornton stood apart from the swirl and buzz of the midnight ball she was attending, watching Lucan Devlin Wynwood, Duke of Mondvale, with the utmost discretion. The *haute monde* found him deliciously dangerous and unpredictable. Constance thought he might easily have been her prince charming…except, of course, he was a degenerate, a dangerous libertine a young lady of virtue should stay away from.

But then, that was one of the things that drew her—Mondvale was even more notorious than she.

She watched his dark head dip as he whispered in Lady Shrewsbury's ear, and suspected he was arranging a clandestine meeting. As if he felt Constance's eyes on him, he glanced up. Her breath seized. Cold silver eyes captured hers before insolently caressing the length of her body. He seemed terrifyingly exotic with his strong jaw, sensual mouth, savagely high cheekbones, and thick raven-black hair.

Heat flushed her body, but she could not look away. Why was he looking at her? She prayed Lady Shrewsbury was not gossiping about her. Constance glanced at the widow and noted she clung to his dark jacket sleeve as if enraptured by whatever he murmured in her ear.

Mondvale had the most unsavory reputation, yet he intrigued Constance. Unlike her, he was uncaring of what society thought about him. He appalled them all by owning the famous gambling club, Decadence. He titillated some, repulsed others, yet they were all too fascinated to banish him from their circles. Mondvale was fawned over, revered even, and Constance wanted to know how he did it. It could not be by virtue of him being a duke alone. Her brother, Sebastian, ruled one on the most powerful dukedoms in England; her family's wealth was unmatched. Yet all that had faded in the disdain society currently showed her. The only testament to her family's wealth and power were the few invitations to the Season's social events.

Constance lowered her lashes and turned away from the cold, magnetic, and penetrating gaze that stared at her.

"She is indeed a bastard! Look at her, the very image of Viscount Radcliffe himself. How did we not notice the likeness? They have the same blond hair and vivid green eyes." The loud whisper of Lady Daphne, the Earl of Wakefield's daughter, clearly designed to reach Constance's ears, had the desired impact.

A sharp tremor of bitterness quivered through her. She refused to show any emotion, trying to draw upon the coldness she had seen her brother display on numerous occasions. She feared she failed abysmally when tears pricked behind her eyelids. She swallowed, but the lump that formed in her throat seemed to lodge itself, immovable despite her several gulps.

God, why am I here? Why did I not tell Mother no?

Constance had been in town for the past several weeks, and after a number of miserable social events, it had taken tremendous courage to attend the ball tonight, knowing the condemnation that awaited her. She felt so branded, cut off, and isolated from the very people who had fawned over and loved her last season.

Only a year ago, she had been one of them, the belle of the ball, her presence sought after by both young men and ladies. She had been so thrilled when she made her debut into society, so excited to go about securing a well-made match. Sebastian had been overly indulgent, declining all offers for her last season. It was a decision she had no doubt he now regretted. Then the rumors of her illegitimacy had surfaced, and overnight she had become a pariah—the Beautiful Bastard. The *haute monde* had deemed her imperfect, and had moved with swift and brutal efficiency to cut off the one who offended their sensibilities. Friends had turned cold, and her laughter and joy had withered.

Even though the rumors also hinted at her brother Anthony's illegitimacy, it seemed that being a *female* bastard was more unforgivable. Yet her mother was still determined she be displayed on the marriage mart. Constance did not delude herself by thinking she was being seriously considered by any suitors. What lord would want to marry a lady with such inferior circumstances? Not even the misters seemed interested in winning her favor.

She had believed after rusticating in Dorset for almost five months, away from the prying eyes of society, the gossip would have moved onto greater scandals. But she had been in London now for almost three weeks, and not one of her many former friends had presented themselves at the townhouse in Grosvenor Square. Even her dearest friend from last season, Lady Annabelle, had been notably absent. Constance had written to Lady Annabelle while in the country, but after her reply demanding to know the truth of the rumors, no further correspondence had followed.

Shame burned in Constance's veins, because despite her elder brother's efforts, even a duke's influence could not coerce people to actually speak with her. The only people at tonight's ball who had conversed with her, apart from her sister-in-law, Lady Phillipa, were the host and hostess. And their reluctance had been clearly evident.

A deep ache burgeoned inside her. Her life had become so tedious. For enjoyment, she had been reduced to watching others enjoy themselves.

"What was Lady Lawrence thinking, inviting her?"

"Her brother is the Duke of Calydon. Lady Lawrence may have had little choice," another voice muttered.

Constance wanted to turn around to identify the speakers, but she focused instead on the dancing couples.

"Don't you mean *half*-brother?"

Her breath hitched. The mocking laughter and twittering grated on her nerves. She wanted to lash out and hurt them as they had hurt her. But she knew a lady did not behave in such a manner. And while her mother had failed to inform her of her true parentage, the viscountess had raised a lady.

With deliberate movements, Constance walked away,

heading toward the refreshment table. She did not have much of an appetite, but she needed something to do. She selected a plate and put a few bite-sized morsels on it. She stiffened as she heard another cackle of whispers from a group lounging idly by. Her shoulders relaxed when she realized for once they were not discussing her.

"He is so devilishly handsome," an unknown voice gushed.

"*Shhh*!" Lady Felicity giggled. "Not so loud." Then she imparted her own juicy titbit. "They say he killed a man in the Orient."

The gossiping ladies gasped in unison, then went silent as if they could hardly breathe.

"I do not believe it," the unknown voice proclaimed, as if declaring it to be so would make it a fact. "My brother says he is very wealthy and a good catch."

They gasped again, scandalized.

"Oh Maryann, only you would dare admit such a thing! They call him the Lord of Sin for good reason."

Someone giggled. "The moniker suits him. He *is* sinfully tempting."

Constance gritted her teeth, for while they whispered about them both, the *haute monde* hated her, yet reluctantly loved him. She who had done nothing to deserve their disdain, while Mondvale actively flouted the dictates of polite society. It was so unfair.

Lady Felicity continued caustically, "Mother says he is a degenerate, and if any young lady were to dance with him she would certainly be ruined. He is nothing but a common gambler. He is not fit for the title. But look at him, one would think he had inherited the title at birth rather than by accident."

Constance's disgust threatened to choke her. An accident? Mondvale had been the next in line to inherit, whether he had been several times removed or not. It was the rule of primogeniture, but apparently that did not matter. She knew what they saw—the self-assurance and the arrogance that was normally only inbred from birth—and they resented him for it. He cut quite a commanding figure, generations of aristocratic breeding evident in every inch of his bearing despite not being an entitled eldest son. She realized it was the mantle of power that sat so easily on his broad shoulders. Not breeding, as far as society was concerned.

"He's absolutely beautiful." This voice had a dreamy undertone of need. "Mother says I must positively stay away from him, and I must refuse him if he asks me to dance. But to be his duchess!"

Constance's lips curled in distaste, for she knew all the mothers were secretly hoping he would single their charges out for attention.

"Father says he's been out of the country for years, mingling with savages and all sorts of inferiors."

"Almost ten years, I am told. He returned to our shores only for the title. They say—"

Unable to listen to any more of their vileness, Constance left her plate on the table and slipped through the French doors that opened onto a wide terrace overlooking the ornate glass conservatory and the stunning garden below. There, she breathed soft sighs of freedom. A slight chill bit into her bones, but she found she did not mind it. It was a welcome relief to feel something other than dread and crushing disappointment.

"Constance?"

She shifted and smiled when she espied Lady Phillipa, Anthony's wife. Clad in a lime green gown that accentuated her lovely coloring and fiery red hair, she looked stunning. Phillipa held out her hands, drawing Constance closer, hugging her briefly. Constance could see the glow of concern in her sister-in-law's golden brown eyes.

"Are you doing well? I did not mean to leave you for so long," Phillipa said softly.

"I…" Constance forced a smile. She knew she failed in hiding her feelings when Phillipa winced. "It is more difficult than I had imagined." Constance glanced through the French doors at Lady Annabelle, who had made a dedicated effort to ignore her since her arrival. "I am regretful I came."

She wondered when it would all end. This was just the last of many attempts to attend a social function since her circumstances were revealed, and it was proving as painful and lonely as her first outing. A musicale yesterday and a picnic last week had been disastrous. She would have much preferred to remain in the country, away from prying eyes, wagging tongues, and the scorn of society. But she kept trying, for her family, especially her mother.

"Anthony should make an appearance soon," Phillipa assured. "And Jocelyn has sent a note. She refuses to be confined at Sherring Cross while you face this damnable ostracism. She and Sebastian will be traveling to town in a few weeks."

Constance contained her grimace. Her other sister-in-law, the Duchess of Calydon, had decided to stay at Sherring Cross, the family's ducal home, for the Season, due to her pregnancy. Jocelyn had claimed to have no interest in residing in the foul London air. Constance knew the bigger reason was to lend her support when Constance had refused to reenter society after her illegitimacy had been revealed, and she loved Jocelyn more for it. Constance had no doubt Phillipa must have written to Jocelyn about her abysmal reception when her mother finally dragged her back to London.

"It will not make a difference," she said wearily. "Over five months have gone by, but the rumor mill is still churning. Jocelyn traveling in her state is not necessary."

Constance's throat tightened in pain. The rumors really had not abated. It was almost as if they were being stoked, deliberately kept alive.

"I understand how you feel, Constance."

"Do you?" She instantly regretted her waspish tone. "Oh, Phillipa, please forgive me. I know you also battle with the stigma, being married to Anthony."

Phillipa had defied convention a few months ago and married Anthony—much to her parents' and society's objection. She had not escaped unscathed, but it did not seem to matter to her. Constance wished she had such a temperament, so she could also disregard society's opinion.

Phillipa brushed a lock of Constance's hair behind her ear. "You have every right to feel angry and frustrated. Please do not apologize to me. I am very aware that Anthony and I are invited to many more social events than you are." Phillipa seemed to gather her composure before she pressed on. "I am beginning to realize ignoring the rumors will not quash them. They seem to grow stronger every day instead of fading. I am of a mind to think your mother might be right, that marriage may be the only way for you to be accepted."

Constance flinched and stepped away. She and Phillipa had become very close over the past few months, and she was the only one in the family who had not seemed intent on pressing the idea of marriage. In fact, Phillipa herself had been firmly against marriage until Anthony charmed her into changing her tune. Whenever Constance listened to her sister-in-law talk about his courtship, a deep pain traveled through her. She wanted that same kind of passion and intensity in her own life. A few months ago, her prince charming had been Lord Andrew Bellamy, the Viscount of Litchfield. He had been amiable, witty, a beautiful dancer, and seemed to hang on every word she uttered. His family had adored her, and she'd been delighted when he made an offer for her hand…at least at first. Then, a few days after the gossip surfaced, he had cried off. Sebastian had been coldly furious, but she had refused to let him insist Lord Litchfield honor his obviously empty words. She was only grateful there had not been a public announcement of their engagement.

She was illegitimate, the by-blow of an illicit liaison. And the heir to the Earldom of Berwick could do far better.

As soon as that bitter thought occurred to her, she buried it, for she had vowed never again to label herself as society had done.

"Lord Litchfield—" Phillipa began, but Constance waved her off.

"Litchfield does not possess any tender affections for me, Phillipa. I asked him, and he just stammered." Since crying off, Lord Litchfield had remade his offer twice. Constance knew Sebastian had something to do with it, but she was no longer interested. "I have told mother I will not marry him if he does not love me. Even if he did…I would not agree, because I know I do not love him."

Constance watched Phillipa keenly and saw the discomfort in her gaze. "But—"

"I know Anthony and Mother asked you to speak with me. I have told them both I will not marry someone I do not love. Don't you see? I want what you and Anthony, and Jocelyn and Sebastian have. The coldness in Sebastian flees whenever Jocelyn smiles at him. Anthony adores you, and it's almost painful to see how you look at each other. Even Mother—" She took a deep breath. "The reason I am a bastard was because of how much she loved Lord Radcliffe. Why, then, do you all not understand that I do not want to marry unless it is for love?"

"Oh, sweeting, we do. It's just—"

Constance's throat burned and she fought back the tears. "I should *feel* something for my husband shouldn't I? Or should I just feel grateful he was willing to marry me, despite my illegitimacy?"

Phillipa walked toward the tables and chairs on the terrace and sank into one. Constance followed suit, and gave Phillipa a small smile when she gripped one of Constance's hands. She wanted only to hide how shattered she was.

"I do understand, Connie, more than you know. And I do not beseech you to marry Lord Litchfield to save your reputation." Phillipa smiled gently as if to remove the sting of what she was about to say. "But when he asked for you last year, you did say yes. I ask you to remember that you must have had some feelings for him and to give him a chance to court you again. And if those feelings resurrect, you could marry him." She squeezed Constance's hand.

Constance sighed. "He is no longer interested in me, Phillipa. I have rejected him twice now."

Phillipa frowned delicately. "I am certain he will offer for you again soon."

"I do not wish to marry him."

"It is unlikely you are going to receive a better offer." Philippa flushed as she realized what she had said.

Constance looked away. Phillipa was right, Constance was unlikely to ever receive *any* other offer. It didn't matter.

Viscount Litchfield was charming when he wanted to be, but it was all surface. The gentle way he had treated her, the laughter, the dancing, and the carriage rides had meant nothing to him. He was shallow, and his supercilious manner of late had certainly not endeared him to her. He had actually hinted that she should be thankful he was willing to marry her despite her inferior circumstances. It upset her to know that she had not seen through Litchfield's superficial charm and accepted his first offer at all. Was her judgment so impaired?

She stood abruptly. She needed to be alone with her thoughts for a few moments. "I have been meaning to visit Lady Lawrence's conservatory. I heard that it is one of the most beautiful in London."

Phillipa blinked at her sudden change of topic. "I will come with you."

"No!" Constance hastily amended her tone. "You are needed elsewhere. I spotted your sister in the ball, and Payton looked utterly forlorn. It is a shame the Honorable St. John broke their engagement. Please spend some time with her instead. I assure you I will be quite safe in the conservatory on my own."

Phillipa hesitated, then nodded and departed.

Constance heaved a sigh. Emotions rioted within

her. She hated that everyone felt she should accept Lord
Litchfield again simply because she had said yes before. He
had cried off, for heaven's sake! And truth be told, a part of
her had been relieved when he had withdrawn his offer. She
knew now, the feelings she'd had for him had been warm
at best, but at the time she'd had nothing to compare them
with. She'd thought those modest feelings were perfectly
right and acceptable.

Until she'd seen Mondvale for the first time. *He* had stolen
her breath away.

He'd been present at a ball she was attending. They hadn't
even been introduced. It had appalled her to know she could
possess such a raging desire for a perfect stranger. It had also
instantly made her doubt her feelings for Lord Litchfield. He
must have sensed something different in her that night as they
danced, for he had drawn her into the gardens and kissed her
for the first time. She had felt nothing as he pressed his lips to
hers, other than a vague annoyance. Which had flummoxed her.
She had been so sure passion for one's betrothed was a real
thing. How could the poets have gotten it so wrong? She had
pulled away, giving him a puzzled smile, then turned to flee.

And ran smack into Mondvale.

Unfathomable eyes had looked down at her, and a
sardonic twitch had appeared at the corner of Mondvale's
mouth. A primal thrill had surged through her, as it had
continued to do each of the four times she had glimpsed
him since that fateful night.

Constance had known then, without a doubt, that Lord
Litchfield was not the man for her. The one positive thing
about her fall from society's grace was not having to explain
her change of heart to him or her family. He'd saved her the

trouble. Even now with her reputation in tatters, she could never marry him.

See? There was a silver lining to every storm cloud.

She danced down the stairs leading out into the vibrant, shrubberied gardens and took the path heading toward the conservatory. She rounded the bend and paused. A tingle caressed her lips and neck, and she held her breath. There was no one in sight, but she felt as if someone was watching her.

After several moments with no movement about, she expelled the breath, feeling ridiculous.

With hurried steps, she slipped inside the conservatory where it was much warmer. She halted. There it was again, that strange, tingly feeling. Her pulse quickened. She knew exactly what it was—Mondvale's gaze upon her. For a timeless moment she was still, hardly daring to breathe. Every instinct she possessed told her he was somewhere in the dark, watching her. The sensation that coursed through her at the thought bordered on fear... combined with a dash of excitement. It took enormous willpower to not flee back inside to the ball.

Where was he?

Close. She could feel him.

She had never known such awareness of another.

But to remain here, alone with him, would be courting further disaster. She turned to leave. The din of laughter and music spilled into the night, but instead of filling her with excitement, dread curled through her. There was nothing for her in the ballroom but hurt.

But the idea of possibly facing Mondvale was nerve-racking. It had been different when she'd only discreetly observed the Lord of Sin from afar, spinning girlish fantasies about her wicked prince charming. Everything about him had seemed exciting, and tempting, and mysterious. Now, he just seemed…dangerous.

She took a few steps back toward the ball and again hesitated. For all she knew, he was watching her from the terrace or the gardens, and not from inside the conservatory itself. She hadn't actually seen him, and the thought of returning to the ball to face the sly whispers and innuendos was unbearable. She squared her shoulders, turned back, and walked deeper into the conservatory.

"Even more curious," his voice drawled ever so softly, prickling the hairs at the nape of her neck. She spun toward the voice, nerves and excitement surging to life inside her.

Instinctively, she knew she had been hoping for just such an encounter the whole time she had watched Mondvale tonight. Now that the occasion was upon her, she doubted her sanity, and wondered dizzily if this daring encounter would lead her into the arms of her prince charming…or only into further ruination?

Chapter Two

Constance had missed seeing the stone bench near the entrance of the conservatory, hidden by shadows and overgrown plants. Mondvale sat splayed in the most insolent manner, his cravat undone, a glass of champagne dangling loosely from his hand. She could sense the leashed power of his personality beneath the casual façade he presented.

A blush heated her cheeks. Was she interrupting a clandestine meeting? From the quick frown on his face, she had the oddest thought that he had retreated here for privacy, and she had intruded. She cleared her throat cautiously. "Your Grace, I… Pardon my intrusion, I was not aware someone else was in here."

Despite the dimness of the light, she was able to make out the curl of his lips.

"Liar," he drawled with an icy bite. It was said so softly, it took a while for the word to sink in.

She stiffened in affront.

Silver eyes slid over her in an encompassing look that was as physical as a caress. "You have been watching me with avid fascination, devouring me with your gaze, since I entered Lady Lawrence's ballroom."

Constance's heartbeat thudded in her eardrums. It was so embarrassing to know he had been aware of her regard. Should she deny his humiliating assessment? It was only half true. She had escaped to the conservatory to be away from it all, not to follow him. "My apologies. I was watching you because you reminded me of someone else." Her excuse sounded inane even to her own ears. His unswerving gaze made her uneasy and propelled her into further speech. "I see now my error, but I assure you, Your Grace, I did not follow you out here."

He gave her a dark, jaded smile, placed his champagne glass on the bench, and rose to his feet, stepping into the light that spilled from the gas lamp in the far corner. She stumbled back, trying to ignore the unwilling interest he roused in her. But she couldn't look away from him, awed by the ruthless beauty of his face. High cheekbones intensified the aristocratic cast of his features, and cruel sensuality curved the hard line of his mouth. He was tall with powerful shoulders and muscular legs, and she flushed, mortified for noticing. He was clad in black from head to foot, with the exception of his snow white shirt and cravat, and the silver waistcoat which fitted his lean frame to perfection. Each time she had spied him, he had always dressed with simplicity, in dark, well-tailored clothes, never with flamboyance.

She found the reaction he stirred in her curious, thrilling—that low tightening in her stomach and the slow drum of her heart when their gaze collided. He had the most compelling eyes she had ever seen—pure silver, making them appear as shards of ice.

She fancied it was his eyes that caused the ache inside her, the desire to partake of the wickedness lurking deep within them. It did not matter that his splendid eyes were partially obscured by dark-rimmed spectacles. They should have detracted from the dangerous aura he gave off, but the slight imperfection only added to his appeal. She found everything about him electrifying.

Caution urged her to return to the ballroom. Her mother would be horrified at her lack of decorum. Her brothers would lock her away to know how she had flagrantly dismissed conventions and dallied with a man like the Lord of Sin in a dark conservatory, unchaperoned.

"Ah. If you did not follow me here, I must assume the pleasures I had been hoping to find between your sweet thighs will not be forthcoming?"

She met the mocking glint in his eyes evenly. "Do you expect me to swoon because you use such uncouth words?" She was proud of how steady her voice was.

She did not understand what he meant by pleasures between her thighs, but she would be mortified to reveal her ignorance. Instinctively, though, she knew it was not a flattering remark.

"If you truly did not come out here to tumble, I will grant you a moment to flee before I toss up your petticoats and take what you have been silently offering the whole night," he said flatly.

She clasped her hands to hide their shaking and curled her mouth at the corners in false confidence. "I reiterate: I did not follow you out here. Nor have I given you any reason to speak to me in such an ungentlemanly and derisive manner. You need not apologize, but I ask you not to measure me by your previous…acquaintances…and I will not measure you by the foolish words which have passed your lips."

She was riveted by the almost imperceptible color that suddenly highlighted his cheekbones. He was blushing?

He executed a curt bow. "Forgive my rudeness. Indeed, you did not deserve my vulgarity, and there is no excuse for my behavior." The intensity in his voice made her shiver. He stepped closer. "I am Lucan Wynwood."

She waited for him to add his titles. He didn't. Which vaguely surprised her. He did not act like the other men of her acquaintance, titled and privileged, all of whom would have emphasized their exalted rank.

She nodded in response to his apology, her heart pounding even harder. That had hardly been a formal introduction. By all rights, she should run from him, from this secluded place, and this entirely forbidden conversation. But her feet refused to move.

Her name sprang to the tip of her tongue, but she could not bring herself to reveal it. He may have heard the rumors. Right now, he was not looking at her with the same contempt in his eyes as did everyone else, and she did not wish to field such a look from him. Nor did she want the look of contempt to shift to not-so-subtly undressing her with his eyes, as some men had been bold enough to do, invariably followed by inappropriate suggestions. Despite his initial rudeness, Mondvale did seem genuinely contrite.

So she used one of her middle names and chose one of her brother's lesser titles as her surname. She told him, "I am Miss Desiree Hastings," and sent a swift prayer to the heavens to forgive her deceit.

At least now she should be able to have a normal conversation, not filled with innuendoes and veiled criticism. She desperately yearned for such normalcy, if only for a stolen moment.

"It is a pleasure to meet you, Miss Hastings. Would you like me to escort you back to the ballroom?" As if he realized what he suggested, he laughed lightly, and she was charmed. "Or perhaps, just to the terrace steps?"

She backed away and turned to wander deeper into the conservatory, toward a table and chair that sat in a brick-paved alcove. "I thank you, but I am most happy to remain here."

He prowled after her. "I would be remiss if I did not point out how precarious it is for your reputation, to be alone with me."

She glanced back at him. "It is very sweet of you to be worried about me, but I assure you it is unnecessary."

He seemed nonplussed as he stared after her, and she wondered what she had said.

"Sweet?" he queried.

She nodded. "Quite."

He smiled faintly in the moonlight, drawing her gaze to the sensual slant of his lips. "You do not consider it reckless to be alone with me?"

Tension crackled in the air between them. "You could always leave," she pointed out, while hoping he would stay.

Surprise flared in his gaze, and then wariness. He radiated such power he should have been intimidating, but she felt inexplicably safe with him.

"I was here first, but I will be a gentleman and depart." He tilted his head and made to leave.

Loneliness washed over her. She didn't want him to go. A waltz filtered on the air, and the words escaped before she could stop them, shocking even herself. "Or perhaps we could dance?"

He froze, then with infinite slowness spun back to her.

She held her breath, fearing and hoping he would say yes. A loud roaring sounded in her ears, but she did not break his gaze. She was being inexcusably reckless, but she wanted to feel something instead of hopelessness, however fleetingly.

A frown chased his features. "You would like to dance?"

"Yes."

She moved closer to him, halted a few steps away, and cleared her throat of the ball of nerves that had lodged there.

He looked down on her, his face neutral, but she sensed he was struggling to decide whether or not to leave. That intrigued her. According to all the hushed whispers that circulated the ballroom, he should have been taking ruthless advantage of her virtue. But the Lord of Sin had not even tried to steal so much as a kiss.

It struck her suddenly…perhaps he did not find her appealing? Horror burned through her whole body at the notion. She could only blame her momentary idiocy on the three glasses of champagne she had consumed earlier to bolster her nerves.

She opened her mouth to apologize for being forward, poised to flee his presence.

He reached out and pulled her to him, melting her words in a soft gasp.

She shivered as a shattering sense of awareness surged though her. Of his height, his strength…his delicious scent.

"I would be delighted to dance with you, Miss Hastings."

"Thank you," she murmured as he swept her into the waltz. Pleasure suffused her. She had not danced in months, and she loved to dance.

She wanted to question why he had accepted her brazen offer. He must think her incredibly forward. But instead, she relaxed, feeling secure in her anonymity. She had already decided she would not venture out again after tonight's farce. She would not abide society's disdain any further, but would insist on returning to Dorset, or to Norfolk, to visit Sebastian and Jocelyn at Sherring Cross.

Therefore, she would make the most of this midnight fantasy, dancing with the Lord of Sin, and hold the memory close, until she felt brave enough to venture into society again.

He twirled her with authority and a surety of steps. He was a graceful dancer, a strong partner, and she felt free as she soared with him. She held his gaze, a smile bursting on her lips. The entire situation was dreamlike—dancing with the Duke of Mondvale as though everything were normal in her life, and he an interested gentleman suitor.

She suddenly wished she had not lied about who she was. Would he have reacted the same way if he knew her to be the infamous Lady Constance, the Beautiful Bastard? She couldn't help wonder if he was aware of the rumors, and if he would have stayed in the conservatory with her had he known. Let alone dance with her...

She forcefully pushed such thoughts from her mind and concentrated on the joy of waltzing. As they twirled, they spun into a pocket of shadows, which coiled around them, cocooning them intimately. The moonlight glanced off the sharp angles of his face, and she could clearly see the dark glitter in his eyes as he gazed down at her. Above them, the night sky shimmered with thousands of stars, and the smell of roses and jasmine perfumed the air. The entire moment was magical, surreal.

When the last strains of the violin filtered through the air, regret curled inside her. She wished the waltz had not ended. But though she badly wanted to, she could not stay out here forever. Phillipa would be coming to look for her any moment.

"Thank you for dancing with me," she said softly, hating to break the quiet intimacy by speaking.

He tilted his head. "Why does a beautiful lady need to seek dance partners in the conservatory?"

Her heart lurched in her chest. He thought her beautiful? It had not sounded like empty flattery.

She lifted her hands to encompass her surroundings with a laugh. "I only wanted a few moments away from the crush. I was told that Lady Lawrence's gardens and conservatory are magnificent and wished to see them for myself." She smiled at him. "Then we met, and I heard the strings of the orchestra...and I could not help being impertinent."

"Ah, so the lady knows she is being bold," he said teasingly, moving to walk beside her.

She was. And she was also very conscious of her gown intimately brushing the length of his trousers as they strolled past a vast flower arrangement displayed on the central table.

"The blossoms are breathtaking," she murmured, caressing the petal of a flower she could not identify. She bent and inhaled its perfumed scent. "There are times when I am awed by nature's beauty."

She was startled when he dipped his head and inhaled

deeply as well, his eyes closing in appreciation of the sublime scent. She glided along the table, and he stepped with her. He ran the tip of his fingers over a yellow flower, and she imagined what his touch on her would feel like.

"That is the yellow rose," she offered into the silence. "It symbolizes both infidelity and friendship."

He gave a soft laugh. "Indeed."

"*Hmm*. It is startling what one can learn when one has an inordinate amount of free time on one's hands."

"And why is it you have such an appalling amount of idle time, Miss Hastings?"

She quickly glanced at him, and saw only simple curiosity… along with something else. Interest, perhaps?

Her breath caught as he gently detached one of Lady Lawrence's white roses with a pair of clippers left on the table and handed it to her.

"And what does this one symbolize?" he asked with a disarming smile.

"Purity."

"*Ahh*, innocence."

Her heart gave a jolt as he cupped her chin, his thumb stroking her lower lip. Her mouth parted slightly, and shock flared through her when he dipped his thumb briefly between her lips. Inexplicable heat curled in her stomach when he removed his thumb and put it in his mouth. Was he tasting her? She had the overwhelming urge to feel his lips pressed against hers.

"Do you intend to kiss me?" she whispered.

He dropped his hand in obvious reluctance. "No."

She squelched her acute disappointment. "Why not?"

"You are innocent."

She furrowed her brows. "I fail to see how they are related."

His low chuckle rasped over her. He stepped back, putting space between them. She moved forward, wanting to maintain their closeness. It was as if the heat of his vitality spread out and warmed her deep inside where she had felt numb for so long.

"Don't you want to kiss me?" Did he find her unappealing? The thought pained her.

His deep wariness returned. "Most young ladies would not be so eager to kiss a stranger. You are in desperate need of a chaperone," he said in a gentle tone that made her even more flustered.

Still, pleasure suffused her that the reason for his reluctance was not for lack of attraction. She could not hold back the radiance of her smile. "I am pleased you are concerned about my reputation. But as hidden as we are in the conservatory, we are not in danger of being seen."

She frowned in confusion when the heat fled from his eyes, and his gaze shuttered. He blasted an arctic chill, one that had her stepping away from him.

"Oh, dear. What have I said?"

"If your plan is to compromise me, I must warn you of abject failure. Many young ladies have tried such a ruse. As you can see, I am still a bachelor. I bid you good eve, Miss Hastings."

Her eyes widened. "Good heavens. That was not my intention. I have no designs on your person. Well, I do…but not in the way you mean."

He scalded her with an incredulous look. "You have designs on my person?"

Heat blazed through her. "I meant, I would like to be

kissed, but I have no desire to trick you into marriage. Please do not worry about my reputation, as nothing is likely to ruin it further." She did not need the look of amazement on his face to know how ridiculous her statement sounded.

She flushed in embarrassment and gripped the folds of her gown. She was being foolish. To be caught in any situation alone with a man known as the Lord of Sin, she would probably have to flee to America to escape the backlash, even if they were not actually touching. "Forgive me. Now it is my behavior that is brazen and inappropriate. I do not know what came over me."

He laughed, looking more baffled than angry. "Forgiven."

Back at the main house someone opened the terrace door, and louder laughter and music spilled into the night. The air felt suddenly alive with temptation as she stared into silver eyes that were no longer cold and distant. They were…filled with heat.

"Perhaps you would honor me with another waltz instead?" he asked.

She nodded mutely. He drew her into his arms, tightened them around her, and put his cheek to her hair. She was thrilled to her toes at the intimate caress.

He moved them gracefully across the stone floor, holding her far closer than appropriate. In their *second* dance together.

Now she truly never wanted the night to end.

She licked her dry lips, and his eyes followed her motion. Fascination grew within her at the slight color that flushed along his cheekbones. A thrill of anticipation vibrated along her spine. Was he thinking of kissing her?

He stopped abruptly, even though the strains of the waltz still filtered on the air. He muttered a curse, and she offered no protest when he drew her closer.

Her excitement roared as he dipped his head and pressed his lips to hers. She tipped up on her toes and wound her arms around his nape. The pressure on her lips was firm and sweet.

"Kiss me," he ordered gently. The desire in his voice wrapped around her, luring her to madness.

"I am kissing you," she breathed, and brushed her lips against his again.

His fingers drew slowly over her cheek, and a frisson of sensual awareness surged through her. "Open your mouth."

Shock froze her, then a wave of heat seized her, making her tremble. "I—" But she tentatively parted her lips, though unsure of his intentions.

He responded with a groan and deepened the kiss, slipping his tongue into her mouth.

She drew away from him, unsettled at the intimacy of his tongue sliding along hers and the startling pleasure from it. "What are— Oh, my," she murmured when he repeated the motion.

"You are ravishing," he murmured in satisfaction, his dark drawl rough with need. "Open more for me," he coaxed, pressing soft kisses to the corner of her lips.

"It feels so strange, but a good strange. Are you sure—"

He stole the air from her mouth, and she forgot everything she had been thinking. His tongue slowly stroked hers, and she gave herself over to the warm, languid sensations building within her. He kissed her with gentle bites and nips, coaxing a response, and she slowly relaxed and gave him everything he asked for.

His hands slid from her neck to the side of her breast. He walked her deeper into the shadows, and she grasped his shoulders for balance as a fever of desire ignited within her.

One of his hands drifted to her hips and squeezed gently. Her knees weakened until she could hardly stand as his hand curved around to her bottom.

She pulled her lips from his, gasping for air, shaking with passion and uncertainty. And a little fear. She had not expected...*this*...when she had asked for a kiss. She had never imagined anything so improper and scandalous. But before she could pull away from the shocking intimacy of one of his hands on her derriere and another brushing her breast, he claimed her lips once more. His tongue mated with hers in long, slow licks, unraveling her from the inside out. His hand clenched her bottom, holding her against him while his mouth devoured hers with smoldering sensuality.

His lips grew fiercer, more demanding, and she felt a twinge of apprehension. Her corset seemed unusually tight, and she labored to breathe. She drew away from him, gasping, and he let her go. What was she thinking? She should run from this scandalous situation. Yet her heart fluttered in excitement. She wanted to step back into his arms and partake of a passion she had never imagined. But she didn't dare.

He seemed to deliberately gather himself. "Forgive me for losing control." He raked a hand through his hair and stepped back from her. "It is best you return inside at once, Miss Hastings," he said with a brittle smile. "I will wait an appropriate interval before leaving, so our absences are not linked."

She nodded mutely, trying to regain her composure. She was thrilled by the night's events, but at the same time, she was at loss to explain why the *haute monde* thought him a wicked libertine. He was a gentleman through and through. He'd only kissed her at her insistence. He had been concerned for her reputation, not just out for his own pleasure.

"May I have the name of your father, so I might pay my address?" he asked, his regard intense and filled with an emotion she was unable to identify.

She went giddy with excitement. She had seen the look in his eyes when he'd danced and then kissed her. It was similar to the look she'd seen in Sebastian and Anthony's gazes when they gazed upon their wives. Constance was not foolish enough to think Mondvale had fallen in love with her, but she realized the expression must be one of desire. He was interested in her. In courting her.

She opened her mouth to answer. And froze.

Oh, lord. She had *lied* to him. About who she was.

Should she tell him her name was Lady Constance, and not Miss Hastings? It hurt her to think if she revealed her true identity he would be disgusted. She wanted nothing to ruin the memories she would have of him, of this magical night. She couldn't bear it.

She swallowed down her bitter regret. "I do not think that would be wise, as we have not been formally introduced."

He tilted his head with a rueful smile. "Of course. Then I will ensure we are properly introduced the next time I see you. Go now, Miss Hastings. Until we meet again."

Constance forced a smile and walked away from him, hating to have to leave. This was the first time she had felt hope since the facts about her shameful birth had started circulating. Hope that her dreams of love and a family were actually possible. And with a duke, as well! If there was a chance Mondvale would seek an introduction the next time he saw her, she would not return to the country. Instead, she would respond favorably to the few invitations Anthony had secured for her.

She only prayed the duke had seen something in her, enough that he would be willing to pursue her hand even after he learned her true identity—Lady Constance, the Beautiful Bastard.

She closed her eyes, forcing her heart to reason, and her mind to think logically. He was a duke, one that would be in need of a wife to be a companion and to give him heirs. An *appropriate* wife. While Constance may be "ravishing," as he had whispered against her lips, and in possession of a sizeable dowry, no man of Mondvale's social stature would willingly align his name with someone as singularly inappropriate as she.

And so, she ruthlessly killed the burgeoning hope, and regretfully pushed the Duke of Mondvale from her mind, thankful she had not been foolish enough to reveal her true identity. That would have been one more heartache she did not need. One she instinctively knew would be far worse than anything she'd experienced to date.

Chapter Three

Miss Desiree Hastings was exquisite. Lucan's usually disciplined body had reacted with painful immediacy to her innocent sensuality. He could not remember ever being so strongly affected by a lady. The huskiness of her voice had washed over his skin like a caress, her tentative smile sending a shaft of desire through him, something Lady Shrewsbury's practiced caresses and suggestive whispers had been unable to do. He should not be surprised, for Miss Hastings was truly stunning. She wore a sapphire blue evening gown, with matching gloves and delicate slippers. Her dress bared the creamy swell of her shoulders, her décolletage, and flattered her exquisite shape. He'd never seen such voluptuous curves on a young society miss before, curves that were sensual and perfect. Some of the more risqué entertainers at his club had such luscious figures, but not as desirable. He'd been struck by the most lurid thought, that her body was made to be ridden hard and deep—lush hips, tiny waist, and more than a handful of bosom.

He'd wondered several times if the chit knew how vulnerable she was, ensconced in the conservatory with him. She had seemed vaguely familiar, and he'd wondered how he could have forgotten such a beauty. Her hair was of a hue he had never seen before, a pale blond that appeared as if it had been burned under the sun. It was those streaks of deeper gold interwoven with every strand that drew his eyes. She was small and sleek, and the raw sensuality she'd moved with as she entered the conservatory had filled him with desire.

Earlier, Lucan had felt her eyes on him throughout the course of the evening. He had watched her watch him, but he had been more discreet. He had wondered at her isolation, and had been tempted to seek an introduction, but had banished the thought immediately. It would never do for him to publicly give attention to a female that was not his quarry. His purpose at these society events was a cold, calculating one, and to be entranced with a ravishing young miss like her was not welcomed. His resolution had wobbled when he had noticed her following him. From her provocative walk to his location in the shadows, he had made the decision to bed her in the conservatory. Lucan had felt a keen sense of disappointment at her arrival. He had not lived twenty nine years on earth, half of his life spent amongst the depraved and the *demi monde*, to not know refreshing innocence. Her vibrant green eyes, a mixture of jade and emerald, had shone first with weariness, then sparkled with artless hunger, and finally open curiosity.

It was the innocent awareness that had waylaid his plan, or else she would have been beneath him instantly, and he would have been deep inside her.

Such a quandary.

He had arranged a clandestine meeting in the conservatory with one of his only three friends in London. No one else's presence had been anticipated. But within moments, he'd struggled between getting rid of her or kissing her. When she asked him to dance, he had fleetingly wondered if it was a trap. Her presence with him alone by choice for any another design flummoxed him. But, God, she had enticed him, and he had seen no artifice in Miss Hastings. He had thought an intimate kiss would have sent her running. Instead, she had returned his kiss shyly, and made an achingly sweet, soft sound against his mouth that had traveled right to his cock.

Lucan took pride in the rigid control he had over his passion. But she had made him behave recklessly. At the thought of her seated on his cock, making those sweet sounds, a surge of pure lust had torn through him almost sending him to his knees. It had taken tremendous will power to pull from her. He had almost bedded an innocent. Something he had sworn never to do.

Just who was Miss Desiree Hastings? She didn't flirt or act coy, as young ladies did in his presence. Instead of being frightened by his crude and crass words meant to drive her off, she had held her ground. Instead of being intimidated by him when he had cupped her chin, she wondered if he had planned to kiss her.

He chuckled. A warm sensation poured through him causing an ache in his chest.

Lucan watched her run lightly up the steps leading to the terrace, her every move embodying innate sensuality. He would find her when his plotted course was over, and possibly court the bewitching beauty. No woman had ever moved him to such thoughts before.

A nightingale trilled its ethereal haunting song in the distance, and he walked toward the sound. He exited the conservatory looking for Lord Justin Bollard, the Earl of Ainsley. Lucan spied him on the upper balcony, or rather, the flash of Ainsley's purple waistcoat, so Lucan made his way under the cover of the darkness to the upper balcony.

"I thought we were to meet in the conservatory," he said as he reached his friend.

Mocking hazel eyes met his. "You were occupied," Ainsley drawled with amusement, and Lucan grunted.

"Which one is the lady?"

A frown marred Ainsley's face as he shifted his gaze to Lucan. "What do you mean? I thought you had already sprung the trap. I saw you dancing with her."

Lucan scanned the ballroom from the terrace with impatience. He had danced with three ladies tonight, and as far as he knew they were all married. His quarry was a young chit. "Who, damn it? I have not been introduced to any Lady Constance tonight."

"But…in the conservatory."

Lucan froze. The conservatory? His gut tightened and denial surged inside him. Carefully masking his reaction, he focused on Ainsley. "What do you speak of?"

Something in Ainsley's face tightened, and Lucan recognized it as discomfort.

"I saw you conversing with her in the conservatory, dancing with her, and then kissing her. I assumed you knew her to be Lady Constance Thornton."

Lucan sucked in an audible breath, one that caused his friend to arch a brow sharply.

"I take it you did not know. Interesting."

No, he had not known, had not even dreamed it could

be her.

A vision of the lady in question danced before his eyes, her lush lips, and desire-filled eyes. She was enchanting, beautiful, and more tempting than any woman he had ever known—and she was the enemy.

She had bewitched him for a few precious minutes, enough that he had almost forgotten why he was here at Lady Lawrence's ball.

The little minx. Now he understood her hesitation when he had suggested calling upon her. It mattered not. Her hesitation had saved him from being foolhardy. But to discover the captivating Miss Hastings was his prey…

This was too easy.

A shame. He had thought he would have had to use considerable charm to inveigle her to his side. But she had made it so stunningly simple, he was nonplussed. He did a quick sweep of the ballroom and spied her speaking with a red haired beauty—Lady Phillipa Thornton, if he was not mistaken. Lady Constance stood on the sidelines tapping her foot anxiously, occasionally peeking out toward the darkened terrace.

Looking for him?

He narrowed his eyes as he took in her apprehension. Why had she lied to him? Though, indeed, if he had known the truth, their encounter would have gone very differently. He chuckled mirthlessly. Just his luck the first woman he'd felt interest for in years was the very object of his vengeance. The gods must be laughing at him uproariously.

Worse, he'd actually entertained a random thought that she resembled Marissa, his beloved sister. The reason behind his quest for revenge.

Not in looks. Marissa had been dark-haired, with hazel

eyes, tall and willowy. No, it had been the hope that shone from Miss Hastings'—Lady Constance's—eyes that hinted at their similarity. A hope he was about to savagely crush.

Discomfort curled through him, and he ruthlessly banished it. The Duke of Calydon, her brother, had no such thought for Marissa when he ruined her and led her to such a painful demise.

Ainsley's gaze focused on him, jerking Lucan back to the present. "The lady is being ostracized. Lord Orwell did his task splendidly. He has hinted in all the right ears of Lady Constance and Lord Anthony's illegitimacy, and encouraged everyone to remember how quickly the Dowager Duchess of Calydon married her lover after the death of the old duke. With a few whispers here and there, the rumors are being kept alive quite effectively."

Lucan nodded. Lord Orwell had gambled away a substantial fortune at Lucan's club, *Decadence*, and was deep in Lucan's debt. To further his own goal, he had used Orwell to full advantage. In a game Orwell had been so sure he would win, the fool had placed twenty acres of prime London property on the table. He had lost and was desperate to reclaim his monies and land.

At the time, Lucan had not been moving in high society, too set on fulfilling the destruction of a previous enemy. But a few weeks later he had succeeded, and thus moved on to his current quarry, Sebastian Thornton, the Duke of Calydon, one of the men responsible for Marissa's untimely death. Calydon had turned out to be Lucan's most vexing opponent. He had not been able to find any weaknesses at all to exploit. But every man had a weakness, and he had been determined to find Calydon's.

The duke had recently wed Lady Jocelyn Rathbourne. Lucan had studied her as a possible weakness to exploit. One thing had been clearly apparent to him on the few occasions he had observed them together. The duke obviously adored the ground Lady Jocelyn walked upon. His eyes ate her every movement, and he looked on her with tenderness. It was not an expression Lucan associated with the man. Everything he knew of Calydon had come only via the written reports he'd commissioned. Yet the reports only spoke of Calydon's ruthlessness, his undeniable wealth, his reclusiveness, his power, and the respect he enjoyed from his peers. Nothing indicated a man besotted with his wife.

Then Lucan discovered Calydon possessed a sister, one he adored. There had been a knee jerk reaction in Lucan's gut, and he had known with icy clarity how he could execute his vengeance in the cruelest possible manner.

It would be a sister for a sister.

The debt to pay must be comparable to the crime. Only then would Calydon understand the nature of his punishment. Calydon would have mourned the ruination of his precious wife. But a sister—he would have wiped her tears, soothed her fears, been there for her from birth. That was how Lucan had been with Marissa. And he knew instinctively Lady Constance's destruction would torment Calydon more. Lucan had resolved that Calydon must know what profound pain and sorrow felt like. And the depth of failure Lucan had felt when he had failed Marissa should be experienced by the man, measure for measure.

Conveniently, Lord Orwell had revealed his hatred for Lord Anthony Thornton, Calydon's brother, because Anthony had foiled Orwell's kidnapping of the lady he had been obsessed with—Lady Phillipa. Lucan had carefully stoked Orwell's wrath and given him the task of finding anything he could about Calydon that could ruin him. Lucan had been both shocked and delighted when Orwell produced a letter the old Duke of Calydon had left his family lawyer, renouncing his two younger children as not being of his blood. It was the exact weapon Lucan had needed to win the war Calydon had not realized was being waged against him. Lucan had always been in the business of owning secrets and trading them. He had instantly recognized the value of the letter and had forgiven Orwell his debt in trade for it. Then Orwell had leaked the vile gossip, and Lucan sat back to watch the impact.

Surprisingly, Calydon had extended his considerable power to quash the rumors, making it known he would limit his business dealings to only those he could trust not to gossip about, or cut his illegitimate sister and brother. Annoying, but Lucan had finally found the chink in the man's armor.

Lady Constance.

She had instantly become all important to Lucan. And he had kept the gossip about her alive and flourishing. For every step Calydon made to smooth out her reception in society, Lucan had thwarted it from the shadows.

"What are you thinking?" Ainsley asked now, at his prolonged silence.

Lucan was unable to peel his gaze from Lady Constance. He now clearly saw what he had not observed earlier. How isolated she was. The vivacity of the woman he had danced with in the conservatory had wilted. She did not feel herself to be part of the gathering. He had thought she was simply aloof, choosing to stay on the sidelines.

And yet, it spoke volumes that the few ladies he had danced with had not spoken about her. They should have been eager to gossip and malign her to any man willing to listen.

Lucan pushed out a breath. "No," he answered at length, "I did not know who she was. No one mentioned her name to me tonight."

"I do not think when a lady is with you they would want to bring Lady Constance to your attention. She is incredibly beautiful. She was considered the toast of the season last year. Did she not introduce herself?" Ainsley asked, curiosity rife in his voice, along with a hint of amusement. "Did she not know with whom she danced?"

Lucan frowned. The lady had clearly known who he was—she had referred to him as "Your Grace." Yet, she had chosen to remain alone with him in the dark. His reputation was notorious. He fully understood he was a novelty to society, the object of their fascination and repulsion.

He, Ainsley, the Reverend, and Marcus Stone owned and operated one of the most exclusive—and infamous—gaming halls in London. He'd been told over and over that a duke could not own, let alone work in, a club. It was simply not done. He did not care. He had owned it before the title was conferred upon him, and he was not about to disown it merely to please society. It offended many that a gentleman's club of such notoriety even existed on St. James Street only a few blocks from White's, but they had all still clamored to join. Because he offered them vice, gambling, music, scandalous dancing women, and the freedom to put on a mask and be themselves in an exclusive club that catered only to the *haute monde* and the gentry's wealthiest.

He turned to his friend. "Yes, well, she introduced

herself as a Miss Desiree Hastings. She clearly did not want me to know who she was." He thought of her laughing eyes and innocent recklessness, and was instantly irritated. "Why is she even here? How did she secure an invitation?"

"You are forgetting her brother is Calydon. And her other brother, Lord Anthony, is a powerful man in his own right, a lion of commerce. They have both used their clout to try and force society to forgive her perceived sins. If not for your interference, they would have surely succeeded." Ainsley grimaced and moved to lean against the railing. "You have had satisfaction from all the other parties who played a role in Marissa's tragedy. Have you considered leaving Calydon be? He is nothing like Stanhope."

Satisfaction? Lucan went cold inside. He would *never* be satisfied. His sister was dead, and until everyone involved had suffered as she must have suffered, he would not be able to sleep, to finally stop having nightmares.

"No," his response was flat, and he need not say more. Ainsley should understand.

His friend clasped Lucan's shoulders. "Calydon is a formidable opponent, Lucan. He controls the purse strings of many prominent families through his investments. And he dotes on his sister. It will be a miracle if you escape unscathed."

Lucan smiled. The wealth he had brought back with him from the Orient and that which he earned from the club matched Calydon's fortune, and it was to Lucan's benefit that he now also held a title the equal of Calydon's. He could break the man just short of murder, with little repercussion. "I cannot leave it alone, Ainsley. Her death haunts me too much."

The earl sighed. "The gossip said Calydon murdered

Marissa, but we know it was not really so. We have her letter saying otherwise." His friend continued, oblivious to the emotions tearing at Lucan's insides. "The greatest blame lies with Stanhope, the man who was entrusted with her care, and you now have him where you want him. The Reverend thinks you are going down a slippery path, Lucan. You are a *duke,* and no longer a common gambler or a shipping merchant. You should be focused on the title, your estate, and on the procurement of an heir. It took the crown four years to track you down. You now have a great responsibility to the realm and to your lands. It cannot be dismissed lightly."

Lucan's lips curled in distaste. He cared not one fig about the dukedom he had been given, or in obtaining an heir. The pomp that came with being a duke was useless to him, unless it played a role in his vengeance. That was the only reason he had assumed the outward mantle of a nobleman and stepped into society these few months. With his fortune and his newly elevated status came immense power. It allowed him to execute his vengeance on those who had previously seemed untouchable.

Also, being a peer, even a notorious one, allowed him to persuade other lords to side with him on issues that were important to him. Since the opening of parliament, he'd leveraged gaming debts and secrets when he wanted certain bills to be passed. He had lived a life of poverty in the seedier parts of London, down in the soot and grime, and in the Americas and the Orient. He had known despair and deprivation. If he could use his status to fight for those who lived how he once had, he would.

All other uses of the title were irrelevant.

"The Reverend would do well to preach some sense into

you." Ainsley grunted, then sighed at Lucan's stony face, and changed the subject. "When are you coming to the club? You have been notably absent all this week."

"I will be there on Friday," he said softly, his gaze returning like a magnet to Lady Constance.

She looked so lonely, standing alone in the crush of the ballroom. She was an important key to his final vengeance, and yet, there was something about the girl he had just kissed and danced with that called to him. Just remembering her sweet taste, the lushness of her frame, made his cock twitch.

Silently, savagely, he cursed his unbridled response to his enemy. *I am weak.* He should feel no guilt at the idea of ruining her. Calydon had possessed no compassion for his sister, and Marissa had been everything that was sweet and gentle.

Lady Constance is innocent, his conscience taunted. The lash of discomfort and guilt bothered him. He ruthlessly banished it. He had worked too hard to sway from his path, to let beauty and innocence get in his way. He allowed icy satisfaction to settle deep inside him. He had already lured in his prey, albeit unwittingly. He would not turn back now. The slipperier the slope, the better. For the harder Calydon crumbled, the more Lucan would savor his revenge.

Chapter Four

Constance felt the thrum of the music deep in her soul. She cradled the violin reverently, caressing the bow against the strings, her heart aching as the beautiful notes spilled into the drawing room. Music had always soothed her, comforted her, and brought untold joy to her life. Of late, the music she produced had been mournful, the notes always too poignant, bringing tears to her eyes. She no longer seduced her strings to play jaunty jigs and warm music. Only powerful songs were played now, the ones that evoked the ache in her, leaving her satisfied, if only for a moment. The last of the notes died away, and she finally relaxed her spine.

"Your new wardrobe has arrived," Charlotte said.

Constance had momentarily forgotten Charlotte was in the room. Staring out the window into the gardens, Constance was unable to dredge up any excitement in this season's fashionable apparel, something that had previously brought her happiness. She had been numb as she traveled with her mother,

and sometimes Jocelyn and Phillipa, to the different shops on
Bond Street, ordering dresses, hats, slippers, and so many other
fripperies without any real interest. What use would they be?

In anger Constance had ordered daring colors—dark blue,
gold, chartreuse, colors very unusual for a young debutante like
herself. Her mother had not objected once. But now that they
were here, Constance had nowhere to go. No friends to walk
with, to picnic with, to attend the opera and theatre with. She
winced. That wasn't quite true. Charlotte was her friend. She
was really Lady Ralston, a widow whose husband had died two
years past. Constance had initially rebelled when her mother
had suggested hiring her a lady's companion, someone from a
genteel family who needed employment. It had stung, to accept
that they had to hire someone to speak with her. But Charlotte
had become her staunchest ally and closest friend.

She laid the violin on the music stand with tender care
and sighed. She stood and went over to sit beside her friend
on the sofa by the pianoforte. Charlotte handed her a glass
of lemonade and Constance pressed the cool glass to her
cheeks. The sunlight pouring in through the open windows
made the room feel unusually warm.

"Would you like to take a walk in the gardens? Today is
so sunny and glorious. It would be lovely," Charlotte asked,
realizing no doubt that Constance did not want to speak of
the multitude of gowns she had ordered.

She took a sip of her lemonade. "In a bit. I would look
at the parcels. I've decided to attend Lady Beaumont's ball.
I do have the most perfect Venetian evening gown for it."
The only reason she now felt some excitement in attending
was because she would see Mondvale. Though she felt in her
heart nothing good could ever come from placing herself in

his path again.

Charlotte smiled at her in approval, and Constance realized she needed to make a greater effort to not seem so morose.

After a soft knock, the door opened and the butler, Mr. Harris, strode in.

"You have a visitor, Lady Constance," he announced without preamble.

"*A visitor?*" she asked, sure she'd misunderstood him. No one had called on her in over six months.

His kind brown eyes smiled along with his whole face. "Indeed," he said and handed the card to her with a flourish.

She took it from him and stared at the calling card in shock.

"Who is it from, Connie?" Charlotte asked, shifting in her seat to see.

Constance reread the name several times until she was certain she had not misread the name printed on the thick cardstock. His Grace, Lucan Devlin Wynwood, Duke of Mondvale waited for her in the parlor.

She looked at Mr. Harris in somewhat of a daze. "Did you make it known that Mother is not home?"

"Yes, milady. I was informed he was here to call on you, Lady Constance."

She gave a weak nod. Mondvale knew who she was? How had he found out? Since her return home from last night's ball she had been conflicted. She had written to him over a dozen times, only to discard the rumpled notes. Each one had started with an apology for lying to him before revealing her name. Each time her nerves had attacked her, and she had started over. She had then resolved to attend Lady Beaumont's midnight ball, and if she saw him, she would be truthful about her identity—and then hope he would not condemn her for lying. But how had he found out that Miss Desiree Hastings and Lady Constance were one and the same?

She dismissed the question instantly. She had felt his eyes on her last night after she had returned inside. That same awareness, hot and almost uncomfortable, had simmered through her. Since he had been watching her, it was very probable he had asked someone about her. *Drat.*

Constance wondered if he had called on her to express his disgust. She suddenly felt ridiculously vulnerable. She gave Mr. Harris a half smile. "Please tell Mrs. Pritchard to have tea and cakes in the parlor, and inform His Grace I will be with him shortly."

Mr. Harris bowed and exited.

"The Duke of Mondvale?" Charlotte demanded anxiously. "The man everyone refers to as the *Lord of Sin*?"

Her voice sounded strangled as she looked at Constance with ill-concealed alarm.

Constance leaped to her feet and paced for a few seconds. *Should I change out of my morning dress?* The simple pale pink dress and the chignon her hair had been gathered in now seemed wholly understated to see the duke.

"When were you introduced?" Charlotte asked, taking the card from her, examining it as if she doubted it really came from him.

Constance could not prevent the heat that climbed her neck to her face, as the circumstances in which they had spoken and danced roared through her mind. Their kiss had been the most exciting thing that had happened to her since her debut. All day, it had been a difficult thing to keep from Charlotte. Constance had vibrated inside to share their magical night in the conservatory with someone, but had chosen to hold it close instead. Now it seemed her secret was out.

"Good heavens, you are blushing, Connie."

She sighed. "I met him last night. We were not introduced. Oh, Charlotte, I lied to him about who I was, and now I cannot credit that he is here."

"You spoke, but you had not been formally *introduced*?" Charlotte demanded, her voice bordering on exasperation.

Constance clasped her hands and forced herself to stand still. "Yes."

"I gather from the redness of your face that something more happened," Charlotte said wryly.

With a groan Constance flung herself into the depth of the sofa. "We danced in the conservatory under the stars, and then he kissed me."

"Constance Isabella Desiree Thornton!"

She sat up, and laughter pulsed from her at the appalled look on Charlotte's face.

Constance hugged herself. "Oh, Charlotte, he did not know it was me. Well, of course he now knows because he is here. What do I do? Do I change out of my morning gown?"

Excitement and trepidation glowed in Charlotte's turquoise colored eyes as she cupped Constance's cheeks. "You look beautiful. Come now, it is best to not keep him waiting. Changing your gown and redoing your hair would take too much time."

She inhaled deeply, squared her shoulders, and swept through the door. Charlotte walked with her, and Constance could not work up the courage to ask to meet with the duke alone. Charlotte would not allow it anyhow. And Constance doubted she had the capacity to face him alone. *Is he angry?*

Disgusted?

The walk through the hall past the library to the parlor was nerve-racking. She opened the door and entered with a serene calm she did not feel. He was standing by the window, his back to her. Charlotte entered, Constance gently closed the door, and he turned around. She heard Charlotte's soft gasp beside her and Constance fully understood. Mondvale was very handsome, in a dark and exotic manner. His raven hair was held in a queue at his nape, and his spectacles did not detract at all from the piercing quality of his silver eyes. He seemed so tall, lean and hard. Dressed in dark brown trousers, a matching morning coat, and a white shirt, he looked supremely confident and at ease. Not as if he was confronting someone he felt deceived him.

His mouth curved into a faint smile. "Lady Constance."

"Your Grace, how good of you to call." She was pleased with the steadiness of her voice. "May I introduce you to Lady Ralston, my friend and companion?"

He strolled over with easy grace, and executed a small bow over Charlotte's hand.

"A pleasure to make your acquaintance, Lady Ralston," he murmured.

Charlotte responded in kind, her voice a little shakier than she probably intended.

"Please, let us sit," Constance said, apprehension and a good deal of excitement clamoring inside her.

Charlotte sat in the sofa nearest to the window away from them. Constance sank into the seat opposite from him, wondering how to breach the topic of her obvious lie and apologize for it. The rattle of the china alerted her before the door opened, and Mrs. Pritchard wheeled in a trolley with teas and cakes, and with efficient movements, laid them out on the center table.

Constance dismissed her and then poured two cups of boiling water onto the Earl Grey leaves. She carefully prepared the tea, feeling his eyes watching in speculative silence the entire time.

"Thank you," he murmured, when she handed him his cup.

She shifted uncomfortably on the sofa. "Your Grace, your presence indicates that you are aware of my ruse at Lady Lawrence's ball. Please forgive my prevarication."

He relaxed into the sofa. "Prevarication is forgiven, Lady Constance. I learned your identity later that night."

She was sure he had heard the rumors as well, but he was still here. Hope surged inside her, hot and sweet. "Why are you here, Your Grace?"

One of his brows lifted in an arch. "I am inviting you to take a carriage ride with me in the park, Lady Constance, if you are available. Possibly a picnic by the lake? It is a beautiful day out."

Her pulse jumped in her throat. No man had invited her to ride with him since she had been back in London. What was going on? Constance thought it fair to warn him, even though she loathed doing so. She placed her tea on the walnut table with a soft clink. "Are you not familiar with the scandal swirling around my name, Your Grace?"

"I am," he intoned smoothly, taking another sip of his tea. "Are the rumors true?"

She held her breath, confounded he would be so brash. "If they are, would you retract your invitation and depart from me?"

His eyes roamed over her, and she wondered if she

imagined the possessive way he did it. It was evident what he noted—the hues of her blond hair, the vivid coloring of her green eyes, the trademarks of Viscount Radcliffe's line.

"Depart from you?"

"Many friends turned cold when they saw the truth of my shame." That was the most she would admit.

"It is not your sin," he said gently.

She smiled in spite of her nervousness. "Are you saying you are not repulsed?"

"I do not subscribe to such notions, Lady Constance. The circumstances of your birth are not a reflection of your character, but a reflection of those of Lord and Lady Radcliffe's."

Relief soared through her, but she could not allow him to be ignorant. "Everyone looks at me with morbid curiosity, and *everyone* speaks ill of me. If you are seen riding with me it will excite the most malicious speculation."

He smiled, barely. Then it was gone, but she had noticed.

"I thank you, Lady Constance, for being concerned with my reputation. Hardly necessary, I assure you. Tongues will already be wagging, as my carriage is parked outside."

She took a delicate sip of her tea, unable to credit that he was so calm about her illegitimacy. It absolutely made no sense to her. "And you do not care if society gossips about your visit to *the Beautiful Bastard*?"

"You are aware of your moniker."

She swallowed. "I would be a fool not to be."

He watched her with something akin to admiration, and a response thrilled inside of her. Memory of their dance and how he had touched her filtered through her.

"I do not care."

Joy suffused her. "Then I would gladly take a carriage

ride with you, Your Grace."

"Lucan."

Constance hesitated, then glanced at Charlotte, who was studiously looking toward the garden, her hands flying as they clenched her knitting needles. But Constance knew her friend had heard every word spoken. She cleared her throat delicately and Charlotte looked up. Her friend saw her unspoken request and rose to her feet.

"I will have Anne prepare your carriage dress and have the cook prepare luncheon for the picnic. If you will excuse me, Your Grace," Charlotte murmured, then gave a small curtsy and departed. She left the parlor door open, and Constance suppressed her smile at the stern glance Charlotte had given her before disappearing.

Constance steeled herself, then met his eyes. "Now we can converse more freely. I am truly regretful I lied to you. I feared you would have turned away if I had revealed my name."

He waved his hands and relaxed deeper into the sofa, assuming a very casual pose. "It is forgotten, Lady Constance. Gossip is not something that would prevent me from inviting a young lady such as yourself to drive on such a day."

Her hands trembled, and she placed her tea cup on the walnut center table in fear she might spill it on herself. Did he want to court her? She wanted to blurt the question to him so badly her jaw ached from keeping quiet. "Then I thank you for your kind consideration, you will not regret my company."

His lips curved into a charming smile, and the need to feel his lips on hers again welled inside of her. She gritted her teeth and pushed the images away.

"It is I who should thank you for your willingness to drive and picnic with the Lord of Sin, the debaucher of all things innocent, and with such enthusiasm, too."

Constance laughed lightly, a giddy sense of happiness unfurling within her. He wanted to court her. It was the only explanation. She searched his face for any sign of tender regard or interest, but the cool manner in which he observed her had insidious doubt creeping in. If he wanted to court her, he would have been clearer. Was it possible he saw her as an exotic forbidden fruit one must indulge in, as Lord Nelson had said to her at last week's picnic? Her stomach hollowed at the thought. It would not do at all for her to get her hopes up. She needed to proceed with caution, no matter how tempting it was to throw her fears into the wind.

But if other gentlemen were to see them together, more offers for genuine outings might come her way. A lady is always seen to be more suitable and appealing when other gentlemen pay her attention. "I see I am not the only one aware of their moniker, Your Grace," she offered with a small smile.

"Lucan, please. I do not like to stand on formality."

"Then please refer to me as Constance, when we are alone of course," she invited.

She fancied it was pleasure that lit up his eyes at her request. She felt warmed, and a little bit flushed. She tried not to stare overly long at his lips. "I will prepare myself for our outing, Your—Lucan. I think cold chicken and sandwiches with wine will be appropriate for our picnic."

He nodded his agreement. "I will be back around noon if that is acceptable."

"It is very much acceptable, Your Grace"—she smiled—

"Lucan. If you will excuse me?"

Constance exited the parlor and lightly ran up the stairs. Life had never seemed so promising, not since the scandal of her birth. A shimmer of excitement pulsed through her and she sent a swift prayer to the heavens that her doubts would be all for naught, that the Duke of Mondvale could possibly be her prince charming.

Her chest squeezed, and she tried to quell the flare of need for normalcy, for what good could come from a liaison between the Beautiful Bastard and the Lord of Sin?

Chapter Five

Constance sat in front of a small walnut table by the window in the drawing room responding to some correspondence that had been ignored for too long. The one she dashed off now was to Jocelyn, assuring her she did not need to travel from the country in her delicate state.

Constance's mother, Margaret Abigail Jackson, Viscountess of Radcliffe, swept into the room, dressed casually in a bright yellow tea gown with her dark hair piled high on her head. She looked invigorated as she usually did after her morning ride.

"Lord Litchfield and his mother will be joining us for luncheon. I have told Mrs. Pritchard to prepare pigeon soup, salmon mousse, lamb chops with leeks, and a pudding," she imparted casually as she sat on the chaise lounge near the window.

Constance stiffened. She was glad she would not be present for lunch and would not see Lord Litchfield. Before she could speak, the housekeeper came in and laid out a few trays with cakes, a pot of tea, and a jar of lemon juice on the center table. She waited until Mrs. Pritchard left before she broached the topic of remaining in town for a few more weeks. "I have accepted a few invitations for the rest of the season."

Her mother paused in the act of pouring tea, her piercing blue eyes observing Constance. "I do not understand, Connie. Are you now saying you intend to stay in town?"

Constance nodded firmly. "Yes, mother. I would like to stay in London for the rest of the season."

A pleased smiled curved her mother's lips. "I am relieved to hear that, my dear. I had spoken with your father about retiring to Hertfordshire, and we had agreed if that was what you wanted, we would travel down with you."

Constance restrained herself from flinching as her mother referred to Lord Radcliffe as her father. She wondered when she would ever get used to the notion. Her mother had been married to him since Constance was eight years old, and she had happily called him Uncle Edward. To now re-adjust the relationship and refer to him as her father was exceedingly difficult. It was still painful to accept that the old duke was not her real father. In truth, it confounded her as to why it was so hard. Lord Radcliffe was a wonderful man, thoroughly kind and gentle. But she felt as if it had been easier when she had only thought of him as her mother's second husband, instead of as her father.

"I am happy you are considering Lord Litchfield's offer. His mother will be pleased to hear."

Constance stiffened and pushed aside the papers and quills. "I am not considering his offer, Mother."

"I do not understand, Connie. I thought—"

"It is not because of Lord Litchfield I wish to remain in London. I only thought to give the remainder of the season a try." She had hoped to avoid this line of conversation.

Her mother sighed. "I know you have some affection for Lord Litchfield, Connie. You said *yes* to his proposal last year. It is unlikely you will receive another offer, sweetheart. And I believe your father is very serious about accepting Lord Litchfield's offer if he makes it a third time."

Constance tried to picture life with Lord Litchfield and could not. He sparked nothing inside of her. "I hardly think I will end up a spinster, Mother. I am eighteen, and I am sure to eventually find a beau who will make me happy. And I may have another suitor," she offered tentatively.

Surprise and hope flashed across her mother's face. "Another suitor? Who are you referring to, my dear?"

Her mind jerked to the kiss and dance in the conservatory. She imagined she could still feel the warmth of Lucan's mouth on her lips. "The Duke of Mondvale called this morning."

Shock chased her mother's expression. "He called? Why was I not informed of this?"

Constance blushed and her mother's gaze sharpened. "You were not here."

"Was Charlotte with you?"

Constance fought not to blush harder. "Yes."

Her mother was not reacting with the excitement she had hoped. Maybe her caution was for naught.

"But why would he call on you? You have not been intro-duced." Her mother could not disguise the shock in her tone.

Constance swallowed in discomfort, not wanting to lie to her. "I met him last night at Lady Lawrence's ball. We spoke. He invited me to the Hyde for a picnic and a walk and I said yes. So I will not be here for luncheon with the Viscount and his mother. I believe His Grace may be interested in courting me."

Lady Radcliffe's head shook with vigor. "Connie, please do not tell me it is because of Mondvale that you wish to remain in town?"

Constance flushed. "Mother, I..."

Her spine stiffened and her lips went flat in disapproval. "Absolutely not. I forbid it." Lady Radcliffe's eyes flashed with anger and determination. "He is not interested in you, Constance. I do not know what he was doing here or how you met him, as your father and I have not made any introductions. Lady Lawrence certainly would not have introduced you! His reputation cannot be taken lightly and I fear his attentions are not honorable."

An awful sensation sank into the pit of Constance's stomach. She had not expected her mother to have such a reaction. She could only imagine her brothers would be the same. Everyone thought Lucan scandalous and wicked. But she had seen the gentleman, the man who had danced with her and had not behaved in a disrespectful manner after his first faux pas. She supposed she *was* like her mother, just as everyone whispered—a *wanton*—to be interested in a man with such a reputation.

She pushed away the shameful thoughts. They had made her miserable these past months, as though she had not lived at all. In fact, if the duke had tried to call on her last year, he would have been met with staunch resistance. She had always had an innate urge to be wicked and free, to do something as daring as riding without a side saddle, like Phillipa and Jocelyn. But the fear of being seen as wanton, and the possible fall to destruction like the one her mother had experienced, stifled any such inclination. It was only recently those thoughts had been stripped away under loneliness, and Constance refused to permit the viciousness of society's whispers to further dictate her life. "I felt alive for the first time in weeks when we conversed, Mother. Though His Grace has not declared any intentions toward me, I am open—"

"This conversation is over, young lady. I will not entertain any thoughts of a courtship between you and that…that…" Her mother visibly composed herself. "Lord Litchfield is honorable. He has a cheerful disposition and is kind. Not to mention he very much wants to marry you. Our families have been acquainted for years, and they have informed Sebastian and your father that my past indiscretion does not matter. You must do the smart thing, Connie, and accept Lord Litchfield's suit."

Heat flared through Constance. "You married Lord Radcliffe only three months after Papa's passing. Why? Was it not because you loved him and did not care about the opinion of society? Why must I be concerned now?"

"You speak foolishly, Constance. I forbid you from walking with Mondvale. He is not a gentleman. He is a common gambler with a shocking reputation."

"You hypocrite," Constance breathed, truly shocked at her mother's stance. "You did not even mourn for Papa! And you lecture me on propriety? I am your lover's daughter." Her voice cracked. "A lover you had while married. Papa is not my father and I found out through *rumors*."

Her mother paled. Constance had never spoken to her in this way. She herself felt appalled, but the unfairness stung.

It was by her mother's actions that Constance's world had been shattered, and now her mother sat before her spouting of propriety with no care for her daughter's happiness? "Why did you do it?"

The silence became profound. She saw her Mother's deep discomfort and did not care. Her actions had affected Constance's life in the most horrible manner. She *should* feel some discomfort.

"Do what?" her mother's hand trembled as she placed her cup of tea on the table. She had always shied away whenever Constance had probed. And she had always relented, fearful of upsetting her mother.

"I thought Papa was *my* father." Constance's throat closed. "You had a lover when you were married, and I am one of his children." It was hard for her to understand her mother, who forever touted propriety, had been so scandalous.

"This is not a conversation we should be having here, Connie."

Constance did not relent, despite the frantic beating of her heart. "I am not a child, Mother. You have never said anything to me except that you are sorry and you beg my forgiveness. I *deserve* to know more."

Tears slipped down her mother's face. "I loved him. I was in love with Lord Radcliffe before I even met Clement, but my father forbade our courtship. Your father's coffers were empty, and my family needed money. I ended up marrying Clement even though I did not love him. He became cold when he realized my heart belonged to another. I tried to love him, Constance…I tried so hard, but I could not. Then Lord Radcliffe was there when I had been so lonely, hurting, when I needed someone, and it seemed the most natural thing in the world to consummate our love, even though I was already married."

The way her mother's expression and voice softened when she said her lover's name caused a deep ache to pierce through Constance's heart. "You did not mourn the old duke."

Her mother wilted in the chaise, all sense of ladylike decorum vanishing from her posture. "I love Edward so much, and he had waited for me so long. After I married Clement, Edward never married. I refused to wait another year or two to wed him. That is why I became Lady Radcliffe only three months after Clement died. Every time I thought to confess to you and Anthony that Lord Radcliffe is your father...I couldn't. Edward and I thought we would have had more time. But in truth I was afraid of my children's condemnation. Never did I dream Clement would leave letters renouncing Anthony and you as his children if Sebastian named Anthony as his heir, or that the knowledge would be made known to society. It is no excuse, for I should have made you both aware of the truth."

Constance's throat burned at the wealth of emotions in her mother's voice. But it only made her firmer in her decision to forge her own path. "You went through so much because of your love for Lord Radcliffe. How can you now say I must settle for something that does not even resemble love with Lord Litchfield? You are doing the same thing society is trying to do to me because I am a bastard, mother. You are telling me I am not worth more, that I should not strive for more, that I must accept what I can get and be grateful."

Her mother's spine shot taut, horror slacking her jaw. "I

do not feel like that, Connie. I only want your happiness."

"No, you do not. I live beneath the shadow of your indiscretion, rejected from everything I have ever known. Lord Litchfield treated me with contempt, and you are insisting that I heed his courtship. I will not. For the first time in months, Mother, someone has shown interest in me, and you are saying I should not entertain his suit because of gossip from the same people that flay me every day. Even if His Grace has no interest in courting me, through our brief encounters, he has only behaved in a gentleman-like manner." Emotions roiled through Constance. She could hardly believe she had spoken to her mother so fiercely.

The gentle closing of the drawing room door had both of their heads snapping toward the sound. Lord Radcliffe, her father, strolled in, his face carefully blank. Constance could see from his demeanor he had overheard their argument.

"Sorry I am late, my love," he murmured as he pressed a brief kiss against her mother's cheek. She in turn gave him a wobbly smile with a sniff.

He turned to Constance, and she tilted her head in defiance. He did the same and pressed a gentle kiss to her cheek before seating himself beside her mother on the chaise.

Every time she looked at Lord Radcliffe she saw herself, yet she had never wondered as a child at their close resemblance. It had never occurred to Constance her mother could have been unfaithful to the man she had thought her father.

"I happened to overhear most of the conversation," Lord Radcliffe murmured.

Constance winced. That was one of the things she admired most about him. He was very direct.

"I will ask of you, Constance, not to berate your mother

so harshly for errors she made many years ago."

She stiffened, words begging to spill from her lips.

He held up his hand, a smile crinkling the corner of his eyes. "We know how much we have hurt you, albeit unintentionally. And I wager we will spend a good portion of time making up for it, as we should. But we all make mistakes, Connie. And the one your mother is making now is out of love and concern. The Duke of Mondvale is no young buck, and he has only moved in our circles for the last year since inheriting the title. Not much is known about him outside of the motions he favors in parliament. Your mother's concern is understandable, but we also understand if you do not love Lord Litchfield."

Constance relaxed somewhat.

"Mondvale has not asked your brother's permission to pay address to you. Nor I. When he does, and we have ascertained his good intentions toward you, there will of course be no objections. We will not oppose your walk in the park with the duke and Charlotte of course, since you have already consented."

"Edward!"

A speaking glance silenced her mother. To remove the sting from it, he reached over and clasped her hand and placed a kiss on her knuckles. He gave Constance a quick wink, and warmth unfurled inside of her. She returned the wink. He had been in her life for ten years, a constant father figure. He had treated her like a cherished daughter, and Constance now understood why he had spoiled her. It could not have been easy for him to suffer her coldness over the past few months. Not when they had been so close. And not once had he berated her, or tried to force his perspective on her. He had simply been there in the background, giving her the space she needed. A pang went through her heart. *I love you*, she mouthed, and she almost laughed as he caught it as he always did and stuffed it in his pocket.

She was content with not partaking in the light conversation between her father and mother. As she watched them, she fancied she could see the invisible strings of love and companionship that bound them together. One day she would love to hear from her mother, in full, their journey. But she knew that time was not yet, and she accepted that. Her brother Anthony had been right. He had told her when they had first found out of their illegitimacy, that what mattered was that they were a family that loved one another, albeit a complicated one.

And that was what she now saw and felt. Family, love, and companionship. And Constance felt more determined than ever to claim a similar future for herself. She would not marry unless it was for love. While she was interested in the Duke of Mondvale she would guard her heart closely until he revealed his intentions. He was, after all, the Lord of Sin, and based on rumors, he was firmly adverse to marriage. More than one young lady had learned that lesson in the most painful of manners when they sought to entrap him. Constance would not be so foolish to make the same mistake simply because he was the first gentleman to show her interest in months.

Chapter Six

After the encounter with her mother, Constance had wasted no time preparing herself, dressing in a dark red flounced carriage dress with matching hat and slippers. Lucan had collected her promptly at noon and assisted her and Charlotte into the carriage and bounded away to Hyde Park. The carriage ride had been achieved with a short conversation between her and Constance. The duke had looked on, the memory of their embrace clear in his silver gaze.

The equipage rolled to a stop and the door was opened by a footman. Lucan aided her and Charlotte's descent. Constance breathed in deeply. She fancied she could feel the sunshine filling her lungs. Hyde Park seemed empty for such a glorious day. A few parties reposed on blankets and she could see two couples walking, chaperones discreetly trailing behind them. Her party walked to a spot by the lake and the footman spread the blanket near the edge of the waters, opening the basket and arranging the food—

chocolate truffles, cold ham slices, chicken slices, sweet bread, a cake, apples, and a bottle of wine for their consumption. Mrs. Pritchard had outdone herself. No doubt the entire staff was abuzz with the news that Constance had a gentleman caller—and a duke, no less. The wine bottle was uncorked, the wine poured, and then the footman melted away.

Lucan glanced toward Charlotte who was some distance away on her own blanket, reading. "Will Lady Ralston not join us?"

Constance shook her head. "She means to give us privacy. I am in her sight so I am properly chaperoned. She also ate before we departed so as not to interrupt our time together." Let him think on that. If he wanted to make his intentions clear, she just gave him the perfect opportunity to refute that they needed privacy.

"Ah."

She stretched out her feet, and leaned back on her arms, tilting her face to the sun. A light breeze stirred, and the smell of the Serpentine Lake and the newly mown grass filled her nostrils. Fresh, crisp, and clean.

"You are enjoying being outside," he observed.

She turned her head and met his gaze. Her heart jolted at the quiet intensity in his regard.

"I am. I have spent most of my days indoors. When I saw how glorious the day was, I really wanted to be out. Your invitation was timely, Lucan. It is a welcomed relief to be outside with someone who is not a family member."

He leaned back on the large oak tree and drew up one of his legs. "I was told by your butler this morning that your mother had gone out riding. Why did you not ride with her?"

Constance assessed his curiosity, wondering how much

she should reveal. From his slight smile she knew he sensed her hesitation. If he did not know how much society had shunned her, she did not want it brought to his attention. But she did not want to lie to him either. If he was considering courting her, she did not want to get her hopes up and then have him reject her weeks later for something he had not known. No, she would hide no longer. She wanted honesty between them. "I did not want to venture out and face another day of malice and whispers."

Discomfort flashed across his face so fast she wondered if she had imagined it.

"It is because of these rumors you have not been out much?"

She bobbed her head in confirmation. "You do not sound as if you approve of my tactics."

"I doubt I will ever understand changing one's actions to conform to the irrelevant views of a hypocritical society."

She had thought the same thing at one point, but how could he understand? They were all she had known since birth. "I do not think you can understand, Your Grace. The title has only been recently conferred on you. I have been a part of this society my whole life. You cannot imagine what it feels like to be torn from all that you have ever known, to bare such hardship."

"Can I not?"

An undercurrent ran beneath his tone, and she suddenly felt foolish at her assessment. She had lived a privileged life. One of the rumors that circulated about him was that he had lived and worked in the rookeries of St. Giles District, the poorest part of London. If that rumor was indeed true, he knew more of hardship than she could ever comprehend.

"Forgive me for even thinking to compare our experiences, Lucan."

He adjusted his spectacles, though they needed no fixing. A sign of discomfort? "Hardship is hardship, Constance, and I can see yours affects you deeply. There is nothing to forgive."

His tone was regretful, and it made her curious.

"Thank you."

"Are you without friends completely?"

She laughed lightly. "Charlotte—Lady Ralston—has become my dearest friend. She is three years older than I am, but we get along famously."

"Are there no others?"

She shrugged. "I have been shunned by those who called me friend months ago. My friends from last season and those I have known most of my life have been forbidden to contact me as I may corrupt them with my wickedness. It never occurred to me that bastardy was so contagious. Lady Annabelle, who had been my dearest friend, now speaks to me with little or no civility," she ended with a forced laugh. It was still a painful topic to discuss, and she resented it had such sway over her emotions.

"Is it important to you?"

She analyzed his serious mien. "What?"

"The *haute monde*, their opinion. Do you want to be enfolded back into their bosom?" he asked, his gaze never leaving her face.

She nibbled on a piece of cold ham, trying to appear indifferent to his question. *Yes!* Her pained heart screamed. "It is nothing of consequence. I do not yearn for it. My mother may dream of it, but I know it will never happen. My brother is the Duke of Calydon, and I am still shunned weeks after the rumors started. There are times I feel as if someone who hates me is feeding the grist deliberately. I am not the only *bastard* in high society, you know. It is hardly such an unusual revelation."

A notable tension shifted through his frame. He tried to hide it, but she saw it. What had she said? Mayhap he found it distasteful for her to speak so casually of her circumstance. The silence was fraught with an unknown disquiet that unsettled her. They ate for a few moments in silence, and on more than one occasion he caught her looking at him. Constance very much wanted to be in his arms, feeling his lips on hers again. She lowered her lashes, lest he see the wanton need in her eyes. What was wrong with her? She knew because of her circumstances she would not be deemed a suitable choice for his duchess, yet she was having such shameful thoughts about him.

"Are you regretful Calydon was not your sire?"

She jerked her eyes to his in surprise. No one had ever asked her that question. Not even Charlotte. Constance frowned. The man she had thought her father had been unloving and cruel, yet she had grieved for him. Grieved for what they could have had, and grieved that he had not been happier in life. He had rarely smiled. Only Sebastian had made him happy, only Sebastian had met his exacting standards of comportment, and only to Sebastian had he shown love. Of course now she understood why she and Anthony never received a morsel of the old duke's affections. Their mother had cuckolded him.

Constance buried the flare of unease she felt at Lucan's question, and tried to shrug it away. "I had been invisible to him for years, more of an annoyance than a cherished daughter. I am not sure if I am devastated he was not my sire. I am more hurt because for years I never knew Lord Radcliffe was my true father. "

"Thank you for being so forthright with me."

"If we are to be friends, I hope for only honesty between us."

His beautiful lips curved, and she wondered if it would be too inappropriate to mention the matter of their kissing. She had hoped he would have said something about them being more than friends. Whenever she had walked or picnicked with Lord Litchfield or other gentleman in the past, they had always hinted about being more than casual acquaintances, flirting and establishing the path of courtship. Lucan was doing neither and it flummoxed her.

I am a bastard, maybe he only wants a taste of a forbidden fruit.

She winced at her crude thoughts and tried to see some positive in their outing. He was here despite the rumors, and the impact it might have on his name. At least he was interested in learning more about her. Even Lord Litchfield had only ever asked superficial questions.

"I understand you have only recently arrived in town for the season."

"Yes, I was in Dorset with my mother and spent some time in Norfolk with my brother. I am happiest at Sherring Cross, Sebastian's ducal estate."

He bit into the cold chicken sandwich, chewing thoughtfully. "Your brother, the duke, he is not in London now? Rumors speak of his reclusiveness," he drawled, and Constance wondered if she imagined the menace in his tone.

"Hardly reclusive," she said drily. "But Sebastian has no use for the frivolities of society. And like us, Your Grace, he is much used to foul rumors being in circulation about him. I wager he finds society irrelevant. But I think he is more enthralled with his duchess now than anything else."

"Is that so?"

She tried to keep the wistfulness out of her voice. "It is a love match you know."

"Is it?" he asked blandly.

"Hmmm," she agreed reaching for an apple and biting into it. She swallowed before replying. "Jocelyn and Sebastian positively glow around each other. I am thrilled to see him so contented. He most assuredly deserves it."

"You are fond of him?"

"I daresay it is the duty of every sister to love her brother, is it not?" she chuckled. "I love both my brothers. From when I was a child they were the slayers of my dragons. I cannot think of better men."

His face closed even further, and she wondered what she had said.

"I have been thinking of returning to Sherring Cross, to the simplicity of the country air." She watched his expression carefully, trying to see if he was alarmed about the possibility of her being too far for courtship. He was frustratingly bland, and the writing on the wall could not have been clearer to Constance. Lucan was not interested in her as a woman, and she slowly started to build a protective wall around her heart, stifling the hope that had been festering inside. She should have known better than to think a man of his stature would be interested in her when lesser titled men were not. She would gladly accept his friendship. But should she try and get him to fall in love with her so circumstances would not matter? She froze as the thought occurred to her. Was it possible, or was she being even more foolish?

"What did you do in the country? I assume your days were extremely tedious."

"Not all the time, there I had a few friends," she said on a laugh. At the lift of his brow she expounded. "When I was walking one day, I ended up wandering for miles. I came upon a little boy, Johnny, and we got to talking. It then became a habit for me to walk that path every day where we would meet by the lake. He was so happy, so full of good cheer, even though he had nothing. He had no parents, no siblings, and he lived with Mr. and Mrs. Benton, a kind, well-meaning couple who cared for children who were left alone in this world. Johnny invited me to visit his home and I did. I met several young girls and boys who shared similar birth circumstances to mine. But they had been abandoned, unwanted by their fathers and mothers. There I was being morose and dour because I lost the regard of people who didn't care about me…and I had *everything*. I'd never been cold, never been hungry, and I had family that loved me. It was a startling realization, and it shamed me."

"Shame?"

She winced. She had not meant to confess that. Her hands scrabbled in the grass until she found a stone and skipped it across the lake. She followed the ripples in the water until it disappeared. What she had felt was deeper than shame; she doubted she had any word for it. It was as if the veil to what was important had been shifted. And she had found herself lacking.

"Until my self-imposed exile, I felt as if everything I ever wanted existed here—with my 'friends'. Balls, the opera, musicales, house parties, fashionable clothes, and even carriage rides. For years I had looked forward to my season, and when I was introduced last year, it had been the most thrilling time of my life. I shall miss it all dreadfully, of course, but I have come to see the shallowness of society, and how empty my life is. It shamed me to know if not for what I suffered, I would have been blissfully unaware of how much others endured, and I really had nothing to be so miserable about."

A spark of admiration lit within his eyes and warmed her. "I see."

He said nothing further, but she was deeply curious about him, a curiosity she found irresistible, and Constance feared she would be unable to keep from prying. Why was he called Lord of Sin and why did he run a club? Did he have family? Was he looking for a wife? She tried to direct her errant thoughts and wondered if she should breach such intimate questions on such a short acquaintance. But then *he* had been bold enough to ask her several just now.

Constance checked her thoughts, as her mother was always berating her for being too forward and impulsive. She pulled her gaze from his tempting lips, wondering how to make him fall in love with her. Was it done by conversation? Or by stolen moments with shared kisses and embraces? She needed to discover its secrets and soon, for she could not abide the idea of marrying a supercilious prig like Lord Litchfield. An offer she feared Lord Radcliffe would soon accept, because she suspected her brothers were wholly in agreement that the only solution for her now was to marry.

• • •

Lucan fought to hold on to his self-control. Constance

intrigued him against his own volition. He wanted very badly to draw her into his arms and devour her lips. He wanted her taste on his tongue, to inhale her scent of lavender and cinnamon, to see those emerald eyes darken with passion. Her freshness called to him and made him realize how often he dealt with the jaded, the depraved.

I have no friends; they have all turned from me.

Those had been the exact words Marissa had written in her letter to him. He should have felt some triumph that he was succeeding in his plan. After all, did he not want Calydon's sister to feel the same pain his sister had endured? But the disillusion in Constance's voice gutted him.

"I seem to have spoken a lot about me today, Lucan." Her eyes sparkled teasingly. "I feel as if I know nothing about you, and I would wager you now know everything about me."

His eyes traveled the length of her body. Not everything. Need coiled in his gut, and he directed his thoughts from the unbidden image of her splayed before him, those sensual hips arched provocatively as he sank his cock into what he knew would be sublime tightness and heat. He would take her slowly. He would savor every touch, every moan, and watch as her emerald eyes darkened with passion and mayhap love. *Love?* What the hell was wrong with him?

He cleared his throat and pushed his glasses firmer on his nose. "I am at your disposal, my lady, what would you like to know?"

"What is your favorite play?"

For some reason he expected the questions women normally hinted at. *How rich was he really? Was he looking for a duchess? Had he really killed a man in the Orient?* "I do not know. I have never been to a play."

She gaped at him. "You have never been to the Theatre Royal? Or the Opera?"

She sounded genuinely appalled.

He flicked a glance at her chaperone, who sat only a few feet away. Several other couples and larger groups also picnicked, and he had seen more than a few looks of complete shock sent their way. Outright disapproval was stamped on many faces. Constance had studiously avoided them, concentrating all her attention on him.

He liked being the center of her sole regard.

Lucan had seen the need burning in her eyes to question his intentions, but she had decided to display some tact at last. He was impressed by her restraint. And that had not been the only need he'd seen in her eyes. The memory of their kiss was forever in her gaze, tempting him to behave foolishly. He gritted his teeth in annoyance as his cock jerked in his trousers with every move she made. He found himself enraptured by the way her luscious lips stretched around her food before biting into it. It did not seem as if the lady was trying to deliberately entice him. She was the complete opposite to the practiced partners in his other sexual encounters, her innocence and natural sensuality was refreshing.

"Well, Your Grace?" her strident demand forced him to focus.

Ah yes, she had been asking where he visited for enjoyment. He could hardly tell her about the hidden fight den Ainsley operated along with their gaming club. Lucan's mind searched for somewhere with which she would be able to identify. "I have picnicked a few times at Hampstead Heath, several times in fact." He did not reveal that this was over fifteen years ago, with his sister. The ghost of Marissa's laughter and her softly lilted voice wafted through him. *It is all so beautiful, Lucan. If only we could stay here forever.*

"But you are a duke."

"Am I?"

"Are you not?"

"I am just a regular man that inherited several crumbling estates and an inordinate amount of debts." The estates were indeed in bad need of funds and repairs, but money was what he had in droves. He just needed to now find the interest to set the estates to rights.

Her emerald eyes assessed him deeply, seemingly probing at his soul. What was it about her that made him speak so freely? Lucan clenched his jaw in annoyance, not trusting the way he had relaxed so easily with her. The push and pull grated on him. Something in him fought to warn her, to push her away from him, to preserve the naive sweet girl that she was. Then a more primitive part of him roared in rage at his thoughts. Had his sister been given such thoughts, such considerations?

Wariness shifted in her gaze, and she frowned as if in deep contemplation, then exhaled gently with a small smile. It seemed she reached whatever decision she clearly battled. "You must allow me to take you to the Theatre Royal in Drury Lane. The Lyon's Mail is all the rage, and I am quite sure you will enjoy it. The sounds, the laughter, witnessing the amazing talent of the actors, and oh the music… You can call on me and we will go together. I am sure you have a box?"

Lucan looked at her in stupefied amazement. He might have not mingled in high society for long, but he was bloody certain no young lady would invite a man out. Whether he was a duke or not.

"I was told there is indeed a box," he heard himself saying, as if someone else was speaking.

"Wonderful," she said on a radiant smile, which had so much genuine appeal, he was charmed.

"Do you have any family you would like to accompany us, Lucan?"

She flushed at his hard stare but did not retreat. His family was never something he spoke about, and only Ainsley, Marcus, and the Reverend knew of them in its entirety. Lucan had determined his life was not fodder for society's speculation so he had held them close. "No," he said flatly, to discourage all questions in that regard.

She gave him a look filled with such sympathy, his chest ached. He wanted to tell her to keep touching him as she lightly caressed his arm in a gesture he was not sure he understood. He did not like how the simple quick touch was so pleasurable.

"I am very sorry, Lucan. It must be lonely not to have a family. Mine is very interfering and tells me what to do all the time, but I cannot imagine life without them," she said with a smile that was kindness itself.

Her satiny skin glistened under the sunlight, her hair shone like gold itself, and the glow in her green eyes tempted him to unwind. A nameless hunger ate at him. For more. With her. And that shook him. He hardly knew her.

"I have a family, Constance."

Her mouth formed an O of surprise. "Forgive me… I assumed—"

He waved away her apology. "It is I who should beg your forgiveness for being so brusque. I do have a family. I have two younger cousins whom I regard as sisters and an aunt living in Hampshire."

Her eyes glowed with pleasure, and he released a slow breath. It did not feel as awful as he had imagined, revealing a bit about himself. He found he wanted to tell her something that society did not know, something not so notorious, and quite normal.

"That is wonderful, Lucan. Why are they not in town, if you do not mind me prying?"

"My cousins are still in the schoolroom, and my aunt does not belong to this society," he said mildly.

He watched her curiosity deepen. She was so transparent in her emotions. She shifted closer to him on the blanket.

"I heard your father was a school teacher?"

The lady was informed. Not many in London knew much of his background. There was a lot of speculation, and some had the right of it, but many had it wrong.

"He was." Going on an impulse he was sure to berate himself for later, he continued, "My mother was the daughter of the previous Duke of Mondvale, a secret she kept from us our whole lives. I fancied our father knew, but he never said anything either. She was disinherited for eloping with him over thirty years ago. She was an only child and as such, I was the heir."

"And when the duke passed on you were found, so you could take your inheritance?" she asked somewhat breathlessly.

"It took the crown four years, but they were relentless."

"A lot of the rumors whispered of you being some long lost cousin, not the grandson to Mondvale himself."

Lucan nodded, though in truth he was responsible for some of that misdirection. "It seemed he did everything to bury the fact that his daughter had eloped."

"Do you regret not knowing him?"

Regret? "I knew I had grandparents alive in the world, though not of such elevation. There had been a time when I tried to find out who they were." When his parents had died, he and Marissa had been alone, penniless, with hardly any food to eat in the winter. He had been desperate enough that he'd rifled through his mother's belongings, for he knew she periodically wrote to someone and watched the post hoping for a reply. At the first visit to his ducal estate Wynter Park, he had found those letters, bound and unopened in a top drawer in the library. Yes, he had regrets—for not having the satisfaction of telling his grandfather what he thought of his callous disregard for his daughter.

"I do not, for then I would not have known my aunt and cousins. From what I learned of Mondvale, they would not have been welcomed in our lives." *But Marissa would have been alive.*

Constance smiled. "Your cousins must be so excited and your aunt proud."

He arched his brow at that. He doubted his cousins cared or saw the importance of him having such a title. While he had ensured they wanted for nothing, not once had they aspired to move in lofty circles, happy with their life in Hampshire. His aunt, a former school mistress herself, was even less inclined than his cousins.

A sharp gust of wind lifted the blanket, and a dark cloud passed over them, blotting out the sun for a brief moment.

"Oh drat!" Constance cried and then started to laugh as a large drop landed on her cheek. "I fear our picnic is over, Your Grace. But it was indeed splendid conversing with you."

She gave him a winsome smile, and Lucan wondered if he had ever beheld anyone as ravishing as the lady. Several shrieks and laughter from the other ladies and gentlemen ensued as the rain pattered with more strength. The footman appeared and in quick time packed their belongings.

Constance and Lady Ralston giggled as they ran ahead of Lucan toward the waiting carriage, while he walked behind at a much slower pace. Something about their joy rattled him. The rain had been timely indeed. He was weakening toward Constance, and Lucan doubted he had ever been in such a dangerous position. The day should have been about using her to discover more of Calydon's weaknesses. Learning more about the man, gleaning titbits society would not know were important. Lucan was a master at sifting through the undercurrents, picking at the details that were crucial, and ignoring what was irrelevant. The only thing he had learned today was how damned enticing Lady Constance was. If he was not careful, she would have the power to sway him from his path, and that would never do.

Chapter Seven

Constance held herself still while her maid artfully arranged her hair so that her golden ringlets cascaded down one side kissing her shoulder, and piled the rest in an artful chignon. She'd resolved to try and make Lucan fall hopelessly in love with her. A quiver of trepidation traveled through her. She knew what she had to do, and she would not falter. Seduce Duke Mondvale, the Lord of Sin.

She was nervous and doing her best to look indifferent, wanting to appear serene when he called to collect her. She had been pleased when he had visited the day after their picnic to invite her to the opera. He had been charming and unassuming and within minutes her mother had been smiling, the dour expression she had greeted him with melted away under his undeniable charm.

The three days wait to see him had been intolerable. She had dashed off a note to him, thanking him for his invitation, and he had responded. At first, when the butler had handed her the letter, she had been flummoxed. She had not recognized the seal—a stunning silver and red design of a lip pressed to an apple. It looked sinful. Constance had gone hot with excitement. She had slit the seal and read the single line nearly a dozen times.

> *It was my pleasure, Lady Constance. I look forward*
> *to our next encounter and shall be sending a carriage*
> *for you at seven.*
>   *L*

Charlotte swept into her room, looking beautiful in a pale pink gown, cut low on her shoulders, her dark hair bouncing around her forehead. Anne put the finishing touches in Constance's hair, and she went over to the mirror. Anne had outdone herself. Constance wore one of the daring new gowns she had ordered from Madame Lemont. A flattering green gown that perfectly matched her eyes.

"You look beautiful," Charlotte murmured.

Constance smiled. "So do you, Charlotte."

Her friend must have heard the doubt in her tone, the one she had been working so hard to bury.

Charlotte turned serious eyes to Constance. "You will be fine. Ignore everyone who stares and whispers. It is expected. It is good that you are going out and not hiding as you were before. But promise me that you will be careful tonight. Remember His Grace has not asked permission to court you, so we are still unaware of his intentions. I know your spirit, Connie, so behave with decorum."

"I will be careful," she said affectionately, kissing Charlotte's cheek. "But don't chaperone me too strictly."

"Constance!"

"Oh pish, I highly doubt anyone can determine if they are ideally suited without a few stolen moments here and there, Charlotte. I only ask you to give me such instances before you hover."

"It is not safe to be alone with a man like Mondvale for even a few seconds," she growled.

Constance rolled her eyes. "Well if someone would explain what I must be wary of, my life would be much simpler. Come on, Charlotte, tell me."

Constance laughed at the fulminating look from her friend.

"We are only going to the opera, Char, and you will be right there. I do not think it possible for me to be ravished under your watchful eyes. Though I doubt Lucan is interested in doing any ravishing at all."

Charlotte released a gusty sigh. "I am still very uncomfortable traveling without your mother."

"Mother has a headache, and we will not make her feel guilty. You know she would push herself to travel with us when it is hardly necessary."

Charlotte harrumphed and pulled on her gloves.

They descended the stairs, hurrying out the door and into the waiting carriage Lucan had sent. Constance dispatched a swift prayer to the heavens, hoping tonight was the night she would be able to unravel his intentions.

• • •

Lucan held himself rigid beside Constance in the plush private box situated above the rest of the auditorium. She was a brave thing. He could feel the tension sifting along her frame. The stares and the whispers were obvious, and he could see it pained her. A pang of regret sliced through him.

He had sworn he could be cool and detached, no matter what temptation she offered. That resolve had faltered when he first saw her this evening. He had waited for her beneath the archway at the lobby entrance, watching as the crowd milled about in front of the theatre. She had alighted from the carriage, looking reserved and more than a little bit nervous. Her lushly curved body clad in a green silken gown only a few shades darker than her eyes. Diamonds dripped from her ears and throat, but the pleasure that lit her eyes and the radiance of her smile upon seeing him, had made his mouth dry. It was genuine.

Now to see her discomfort when she should be enjoying herself affected him. Acting on impulse, he slipped his hand over hers and laced her fingers through his. Her head dipped, and she stared at their intertwined fingers for long frozen seconds.

Lucan considered her bent head, wondering if he had made a gross miscalculation. Probably his attentions were not as welcome as he had thought. He had seen wariness in her eyes on more than one occasion and that would not do at all. He needed her close, vulnerable, not hiding behind any protective walls. She lifted her head, and the smile she bestowed upon him punched him in his solar plexus. It was the only explanation for how the breath escaped from his lips.

She subtly shifted closer to him, and he felt when the tension leaked out of her frame. He was very conscious of Lady Ralston seated behind him, and he was happy for her presence, for he could see himself doing something highly inappropriate in the darkened box. Like trailing his hands beneath Constance's petticoats to find out if the passion she exuded when dancing and kissing extended to everywhere. He could imagine her, spread wantonly, tangled in the sheets on his bed beneath him, making those aroused sounds as he drove deep into her. He grimaced as his trousers tightened in discomfort. He determinedly pushed the images from his mind and examined the many ladies aiming disapproving stares their way.

Many matrons of society shone their opera glasses and blatantly ogled them. Lucan knew he was gossiped about and that many wondered about him. But it had never been as obvious to him as tonight. For tonight he was sharing his box with *the Beautiful Bastard*. A sharp sense of uneasiness plagued him. It affected him too deeply, knowing of her pain.

The curtains drew, and she sat forward, a soft smile tilting the corners of her lips. He thought back to the report he had on her. When the season had opened, her family had made a show of support, and everyone had stepped out. Calydon and his duchess, Lord Anthony and Lady Phillipa, and Lord and Lady Radcliffe. Yet Constance had not stayed in London. After only a few outings, she had retreated to the country. Where she apparently only took long walks, visited her brother's tenants, and became a patron to a kind and charming old couple that cared for unwanted children.

Lucan could not identify with the pain she felt at society's shunning. Society's opinion had never mattered much to him. But it certainly had mattered to his sister. Marissa's many letters of how society had treated her when it had been revealed she was Calydon's mistress had been filled with pain and grief. Friends had stopped calling on her, her husband had beaten her and turned her away, cutting off her allowance. She'd had no one, and those letters reached him months after she had needed him. That familiar feeling of rage started to creep over him and with cold determination he pushed those memories away.

The play started and after a few minutes he found himself immersed in the raw talent of the people below. He chuckled at the irony, as the play itself revealed to be one of revenge and lost love. How apt. He was able, for almost an hour, to leave the cares of the world behind and relax into a world of greasepaint and artifice.

The lights came on as the interval was announced. Laughter and noises danced on the air. Lady Ralston announced she was visiting the ladies' withdrawing room, and departed after giving her charge a stern look. He raised his brow at the wink he saw Constance gave her.

She glanced at him, smiling. "Charlotte fears for my virtue. I cannot imagine what she believes could happen here in a sea of people."

He glanced around the box, and the drawn curtains. He could imagine a lot. Especially while the play was in progress. The complete darkness was an unbearable temptation.

She gave him an expectant look. "Is it not wonderful, Lucan? I am not sure where is more splendid, here or the Royal Italian Opera at Covent Garden. They are my two favorite places to visit. I love the arts, music, acting. I insist you visit both."

"I certainty will, if you will grace me with your presence when I do."

Her eyes glowed with obvious delight. "I have been wondering, Lucan... What is it that you do for simple enjoyment?"

He assessed the curiosity on her face. "I run a club."

"The note you had delivered to me...the seal had the design of a pair of lips kissing an apple. I assume that is not the Mondvale seal."

She vibrated with excitement, and he found once again he wanted to share something of himself with her.

"No, it was not. It was the seal of my club, Decadence, meant to represent the temptations to be had upon entrance."

"What kind of temptations?"

"Vices you wouldn't understand."

"You would be surprised what I can understand, Your Grace," she drawled.

He chuckled, then relented. "I give our patrons the opportunity to pursue a life of extravagant indulgence without condemnation."

"Tell me more," she prompted relaxing in her chair. Noting his hesitation no doubt, she touched his arm. "If you fear for my sensibilities, I will happily hear something else about you."

She waited with an air of expectation, and Lucan was confounded as to what to say. She was too damn innocent. He had spent years in filth, in poverty, among prostitutes and swindlers. A world she could not imagine. He had gotten his first job at fourteen in the dock yards after his parents' untimely death in a carriage accident, having the responsibility of caring for Marissa who had been one year younger. While she lived in the country, he had been working more jobs than he could remember in London, sending money back for her upkeep. By the time he had reached nineteen, his aunt had tracked him down and offered him an opportunity at life. By twenty he invested in a shipping venture, which had proven to be more than lucrative, and he had set sails away from England determined to make something of his life for his family.

He found himself wanting Constance to know about him, but damn if he knew what he could safely disclose. "There is not much to tell. My business interests are numerous. I have traveled extensively—the Orient, India, and the Americas."

She scrunched her face in disappointment. "Is that all you have to offer?"

"I fear so," he said drolly.

"I do not believe you," she countered, a teasing expression on her face. "Whispers of your licentiousness are vaunted."

"I had not thought you a young lady who would believe every piece of gossip uttered."

She drew in a sharp breathed and flushed. "Forgive me."

He shook his head. "No, that was uncalled for. It is not every day I am reminded of my notoriety so artlessly."

She gave him a tentative smile. "Everyone speaks about you and your club, and I fear I was in a position to overhear a few times. It all sounds grand and mysterious. I heard how exclusive membership is and that everyone has a unique ring designed for them that gives them entrance."

She had indeed heard a lot.

"I think I would like to visit one day. I am sure the opulence and the splendor I have heard spoken about in hushed whispers are true."

Lucan laughed. "I assure you if an innocent like you were to visit, you would find yourself without any virtue before the night finished."

Wariness flared in her eyes, and he thought it was about time he saw it. The little minx was too reckless. Then her lovely brow arched and the caution melted away. "I believe you are not as unprincipled as you would have me believe. I am confident you would not allow anyone to take such advantage of me."

He stared at her in amazement. "*I* am the one you would be in danger of, Lady Constance, not any of my patrons."

"Oh!"

Instead of the blush he had expected, he got a slow smile that dazzled him.

"Then I positively must visit one day, in secret of course."

He wondered fleetingly if he had heard correctly. But from the challenging way she stared at him, he knew she had really said such words.

"As you are without a ring, and I assure you, it would be impossible for you to obtain one, I must give you the secret code."

As expected, she straightened. "There is a secret code to gain entrance? I have not heard of this, and I now believe you are simply jesting with me."

Lucan smiled at her excitement. "There is such a code. Once you mention it, it gives you carte blanche. Only five people know that word, my lady."

She grinned in apparent scandalized delight. The way he watched for the laughter to shine in her eyes and the curve of her lips was damnably irritating.

"And what token must I give to learn this code?" she asked archly.

His gaze dipped to her lips, which she was biting worriedly between her teeth.

"Are you thinking of kissing me, Lucan?" she blurted.

He snapped his gaze to meet her curious stare. "No," he

answered tersely.

"You have been looking at my lips," she pointed out. "And I would happily surrender a kiss for the secret code, not that I will ever be able to use it."

As if on cue, his gaze dropped back to her lips, and he had to forcibly glance away from their beckoning lushness. Lucan smiled at the humor dancing in her eyes. The minx was teasing him. What was it about her that was so enticing?

He was only eleven years older, but the gap in their experience made him feel ancient, like a despoiler of innocence. He gritted his teeth. That was exactly what he was setting himself up to be, even though he wanted nothing more in life at this moment than to kiss her again.

He felt doomed.

• • •

The play restarted and Constance's fingers laced with Lucan's, her heart beating in anticipation. She held her breath, hoping he would kiss her and uncaring that Charlotte would return at any moment. Constance had spied her stopping at Lady William's box, several rows below their balcony, and had prayed Charlotte would stay there for a while. Lucan spoke so freely when they were alone, and Constance wanted nothing to interrupt it.

"Will you ignore my assessment, Lucan, or do the gentlemanly thing and confess the truth of my statement? Or is it possible you are afraid for me to have the secrets to Decadence?"

Subtle challenge lit his eyes. "You are a fearless little thing aren't you?"

Before fear could rule her and common sense won

out, she spoke. "I only thought you might want to kiss me again." She had caught him several times glancing at her lips, and each time tension had seemed to tighten his frame. It had occurred to her after a while, that maybe he had been thinking about their kiss in the conservatory as much as she had.

"You play a very dangerous game, Lady Constance."

She faltered at the undercurrent in his voice. "I am being too bold, aren't I? Young ladies do not tease gentlemen about kissing them." She hesitated and then pressed on. "I never figured you to be so prudish; you are after all the Lord of Sin."

He threw back his head, and she loved that she made him laugh. Was she insane? This was the second time she had made such inappropriate remarks. It was as if he brought out the worst in her, or was it the best? She only knew she was certainly behaving in a most scandalous fashion. A voice in her heart whispered that it was because of her illegitimacy. She was not proper at all, so why should she pretend?

She searched for a safe topic before she did something as reckless as pulling his head down to hers to kiss him. She wouldn't be able to bare the hurt when he rejected her. "Isn't Her Majesty's theatre grand? I think your cousins would be thrilled to be here."

"They are too content with learning the secrets of Woodbury Park for anything in London to appeal."

"*The* Woodbury Park?"

"Yes."

It was a magnificent estate, and well known to her, possessing some of the finest acreage in Hampshire. Sitting on two hundred acres of prime grounds, with one hundred rooms, and with a lake revered for its wealth of fishes, the estate had been coveted. The earl that had owned it before had had to sell it to cover his debts. Her brother Anthony had a love for purchasing old estates and restoring them and had wanted Woodbury Park, but someone had purchased it before he had been able to make an offer. "It is a beautiful home. I certainly understand their happiness to stay in the country. I feel most relaxed and unburdened when I am surrounded by nature and such effortless beauty."

His eyes dropped to her lips, and his sliver orbs blazed with an indecipherable emotion.

"Indeed," he murmured.

"I really do believe you are thinking of kissing me, Your Grace," she said on a whisper, heat curling through her at his soft chuckle and intent regard.

"You are a danger to yourself," he muttered, then drew her to him.

The heat of his hand burned her shoulders. His gaze locked with hers and desire shimmered in the air. Something shifted over his face, and she trembled. He wanted her. Constance was sure of it. So why did he hesitate? Her lips tingled with the need to kiss him; did he not feel the same? "Why are you waiting?"

He tensed, then released her.

The hurt that pinged inside switched to annoyance when he chucked her against her chin as her brothers did. She did not want him to possess brotherly affections for her. It could not be so after how he had ravished her mouth before. Was he trying to put distance between them? After all, she was the one who suggested they kiss—twice! Shame scorched her and Constance sucked in a harsh breath. "I...I...misread the situation. I am mortified, I…I thought us being here that—"

Lucan leaned forward and his lips swallowed the rest of her inarticulate stammer. Relief eased the tension from her frame. *He wants me.* The sensual thrust of his tongue into her mouth set her body alight with wanton desire, and she eagerly responded. He kissed her slowly, deeply, without the raw passion of their first kiss, but somehow it was sweeter, more thrilling.

It was over before it even started as he gently pulled away from her. His breathing was ragged as he spoke. "Behave yourself." Then as if he could not help himself, he placed another quick kiss on her lips and then whispered. "Revenant."

The curtain to the box parted as he leaned back in his seat and Charlotte swept inside. Constance could feel her friend's gaze on her, and she was thankful the box was darkened enough to hide her flushed face.

She had felt a sliver of doubt earlier that she could really make him fall in love with her. Her illegitimacy was always in her mind, though she promised herself she would not dwell on it. She had seen her brother Anthony ravaged by similar doubts when he had fallen in love with Phillipa. Who would really want to align themselves with the Thornton's bastards? The stain on the person's reputation and honor would be irreversible. But Phillipa had still fought for Anthony, and Constance slowly started to realize Lucan could not want to take advantage of her perceived inferior connection. Many of the young men from last season had wasted no time in being improper, but Lucan had only behaved like a gentleman. He had made no lurid suggestions, and it was at her teasing he'd relent and kissed her. She wished she knew the reasons he had not declared his intentions, but for the first time she considered her illegitimacy may truly not matter to him. She thought of all the signs Phillipa had told her that indicated a man's interest.

He couldn't stop staring at her. Check.

He smiled whenever she smiled. Check.

He laughed when she was being silly. Check.

He kissed her. Check twice.

She frowned in consternation. Phillipa's exact words had been "when a man is falling in love with you, he won't be able to stop himself from kissing you". Constance steadfastly discounted the fact that she had hinted for Lucan's kisses. What mattered was that he had been unable to prevent himself from kissing her.

And best of all, he had given her the secret code. She was sure that was the word he had whispered against her lips. *Revenant.* He was a charming rogue who made her head spin and her heart giddy with excitement. Constance resolved then that she would not be the one to initiate an intimate embrace between them again. She wanted to be without illusion of Lucan's regard for her. But she certainly would discreetly allow for ample opportunities if Lucan wanted to steal kisses after he declared himself. She sighed and sank into the cushions, pleased with herself. She was determined to plan her siege of his heart carefully, for she feared she was already losing hers to him.

Chapter Eight

Lucan was dragging his feet. His plan to ruin Calydon had not allowed for him to be in Constance's presence so much. A few days at most should have been sufficient for him to determine how he would use her to destroy Calydon. And that was the problem. Lucan knew how exactly, but he was reluctant. She had sent him a thank you note after the theatre. To which he had responded with an invitation to the Royal Italian Opera, and teased he held more secrets of *Decadence* to which she held the bartering chips. That had started a written banter between them, which had now become the norm for them between outings. He had seen her a few times since the opera, and she only drew him further into her spell. They had visited the splendid Kew Gardens and the Royal Academy of Music, where she hoped to attend one day. He learned the lady's interests were vast and that she spoke several languages. She was refreshingly honest, and kind to a fault. Strong, too. Many young ladies would have already buckled under the disparagement of society.

Erotic visions of taking her also tended to keep him restless deep into the dark hours of the nights. The ones that scared the hell out of him weren't the sexual visions of her riding him slowly, of seeing Constance on her knees, her lush hips and back arched in the most sensual manner to take him. No, those visions tied him in hot chains of lust and need. The ones that petrified him were when he dreamed of laughing with her, reading a book and having a lively discussion before the fire, of seeing her swollen with his child, strolling by the lake. He imagined her green eyes challenging him, teasing him, and the feelings that encompassed him had been more intense than what filled him when he thought of making love with her. The lady was dangerous. Lucan needed to keep a safe and emotional distance. No more touching, and certainly no more kissing, despite the cravings in his body and soul. He needed that damn distance if he ever hoped to succeed in ruining Calydon.

It is not your sin.

Lucan closed his eyes against the words he had uttered to Constance. He had not known he would say such a thing to her until they spilled from his lips. But they had slapped him with the truth, and it was an ugly truth he had forced himself to consider over the past few days. The sins of Calydon were not hers to bear.

Marissa's life had been forfeited way before her time, at the tender age of twenty-two, and Calydon had been the one to execute it surely as if he had put the rope around Marissa's throat. But was it Constance's sin? Lucan could not seem to pacify his growing disquiet. He had been so sure of his path of vengeance, so undoubting. Now a mere slip of a girl was enough to shake his resolve. It angered him that he could be so easily swayed from years of plotting. And for what? Pleasure? To taste her lips again?

"Please, Your Grace, I beg of you. Have some mercy," the sobbing voice pleaded. "I will find means to pay my debts, I swear to you, Your Grace."

Lucan gazed at the pitiful form of William McFarlane, Earl of Stanhope, his late sister's husband. Several months ago Stanhope had not been pitiful. Far from it. He had been living a lavish life style, one of wild decadence. He had gambled heavily, certain with a roll of the dice, he would regain his fortune. Lucan had extended credit to the man for months, despite his mounting debts. And when Lucan owned all of Stanhope's non-entailed properties—his lands, horses, and possessions—Lucan called in the debts, and revoked Stanhope's entrance into his club. Lucan had ensured Stanhope would never see wealth again.

Nothing Lucan could do would atone for his sister's death. Nothing would bring her back. But each man that contributed to her downfall would surely pay, and Stanhope was the guiltiest of them all. He had brutally beaten Marissa until she had taken her own life to escape. Lucan held Stanhope's gaze. "Marissa Alicia Wynwood," Lucan said without an ounce of emotion.

Understanding was slow in coming, but when it came, all the blood leeched from Stanhope's face, and he sunk to his knees. With a twist of his lips, Lucan turned and walked out of the man's townhouse, deaf to his wails and pleas for forgiveness. He had only visited because he wanted the man to understand the reasons for his downfall.

Lucan exited without fanfare and jumped into his waiting carriage. His driver knew exactly where to carry him, and they rumbled into motion. No, he would show no mercy to all who had participated in Marissa's ruin. He had already claimed vengeance on two of the men responsible for her demise. And in a very similar manner, Calydon would be the last. Lucan would not be swayed. No matter how tempting it was to pursue a different path with a green-eyed beauty.

• • •

An hour later, Lucan stood in bleak stillness in Kensal Green Cemetery, immune to the cold gust of wind at his sister's grave. He stared at the carved letters on the monument: Marissa's name, her date of birth and death—the sum of her existence. No withered flowers other than his to show anyone thought of her beyond the foul rumors that whispered of her demise.

Even now, years later, he could still unearth the whispers that had tainted her name. Marissa the pure, Marissa the lovely, had slowly become Marissa the mistress, Marissa the abandoned. Misused and abandoned by The Duke of Calydon.

When Lucan had started his hunt, old gossips had surfaced of the duke himself being her murderer and people were sure he had strangled Marissa with his own hands. Lucan heard of how Calydon had fought with Lord Stanhope in his country home over Marissa. Then later when Calydon had been spurned, they said he had killed her. Then the rumors changed, insisting Lady Stanhope had killed herself. Lucan, however, knew the full truth; he had dozens of her letters, which he read over and over again.

"You are tormented by the path you have taken," the Reverend murmured.

Lucan grunted and placed the flowers on the grave.

After saying a quick prayer, he walked off and the Reverend followed beside him silently.

"I had never thought it would be so. Is it because of Lady Constance?"

Lucan glanced at Westbrook, the second man he called friend and his partner in *Decadence*. Their relationship was very much a paradox. Westbrook was the rector at Lucan's ducal seat in Suffolk. They were childhood friends who had known hardship and pain together. So when Westbrook had approached Lucan for the post, he had simply appointed Westbrook rector, despite Lucan's surprise his friend desired such a position in life. He knew Westbrook understood about demons and wanting redemption for past failures, so Lucan never hesitated. Before he could even begin to formulate and express how Constance made him feel, Westbrook spoke.

"Since your return to London I have never seen you so free, so relaxed."

Lucan grunted, unable to refute Westbrook's observation.

"Are you still adamant on making Calydon pay?"

"I cannot release him from his debt."

"No one forced Marissa to do what she did, Lucan," Westbrook pointed out firmly. It was not the third or fourth time his friend had tried to make him see reason with that argument. But Lucan saw clearly enough. He was without illusions. They *all* failed her, and Lucan may have been the greatest culprit of them all, for he had not saved her. He had read the unhappiness in her letters, seen the path of destruction she had been on. But he had stayed in India, then sailed to the West seeking his fortune, thinking that was what she needed to be happy. He should have dropped everything and come home for her. Now he had more wealth than he could use in his lifetime, and she was far beyond his help. Nothing he could do would atone for her death, but he could ensure every party suffered.

He ignored the taunting whisper of his conscience proclaiming Constance to be blameless. God, she was beautiful. He did not like how she appealed to him. To court vengeance against Calydon would be to ruin Constance. Something Lucan doubted he could do. As if Marissa heard him from the grave, the yew trees rustled and swayed under a powerful gust, and the wind whistled a long mournful cry into the night. No, he could not turn back. He would not fail her so completely. But he could not bring himself to do what Calydon had done to Marissa. Woo her, bed her, and then abandon her.

Constance was too innocent. Lucan promised himself then and there, no matter the temptation, he would not make love to her. He gritted his teeth even as his body surged in denial. She was so responsive, her kisses so sweet and enticing. He hungered to be inside her more than how he had ever done with any other woman. And he feared he would never feel such a visceral desire for anyone again. But he would leave her untouched by him at least in that regard. He was a blackguard, but he was not that far gone.

He closed his eyes against the ache that bloomed inside his chest. He would have to execute his revenge against Calydon soon. He moved ahead of time, but he had to do so. Constance tempted him too much. He had to act now, or fall into her lures so deeply he would abandon his plans and fail his sister all over again.

Chapter Nine

Constance knew without a doubt Lucan was the man for her. She luxuriated in the thrilling knowledge. He was not exactly how she had dreamed her prince charming would be. She had always imagined someone fairer, closer to her own height, someone with a sweet and amiable disposition. She did not believe Lucan was of a sweet disposition. He was too intense. But he was a gentleman, kind and caring of her sensibilities, and he roused sensations and needs in her she had not thought possible. In short, he was absolutely perfect. She had determined she would not leave tonight's ball without full knowledge of his intention toward her. A bold undertaking, but she was resolute. Her mother kept pressing her to accept Lord Litchfield's hand and with the belief only marriage could salvage Constance's reputation, her mother would soon convince her father and brothers of Litchfield's suit.

Constance had ensured she would look fetching as she

faced Lucan tonight. She wore a brilliant satin burgundy gown. Her hair was bound tightly, with plaits wrapped around her head like a crown, and it glittered with multitudes of golden threads. Her red satin dancing slippers sparkled under the chandeliers as she swept from the stifling heat of Lady Beaumont's ball. It was a rousing success and the crush was more than Constance could bear. And as she stepped outside, she took a deep breath of the cool night air.

But her true reason for leaving had been seeing Lucan exiting through the side doors. She slipped outside into the gardens knowing she would have only a few moments before being found by her mother or Charlotte. Constance walked with nimble steps down the stone path and then paused. She was so sure the intent look he had given her before he slipped away had meant that she should follow him. She bit her lip, wondering if she was being silly. What if he had gone into the garden to meet with someone else?

She dismissed the thought instantly. He was a gentleman. He would never walk and share such kisses with her if he was interested in someone else. She rounded the bend and stepped into the garden. Its enclosure was intimate and secluded, and she saw no one. She walked a bit further into the garden and as she turned to return inside, she saw him standing at the edge of a bush.

He stepped from the shadows with a look on his face she had never seen on him before. It was intent and piercing. A scowl settled on his face. "Why did you come out here, Constance?"

Her heart sank. She had obviously misread his signals, but it mattered not. She needed to speak with him. She walked deeper into the gardens toward the stone benches. "I thought you meant for us to meet here. I noticed you had not sought me out for any dances. I thought mayhap you wanted to dance under the stars again." He had not approached anyone else, either, but she thought it unusual given the attention he had been showing her. Even this morning, her mother had remarked upon how often His Grace called upon her for outings. Constance knew she was being forward, but she fancied they had at least become friends, and she needed to know if he wanted *more* than friendship.

He thrust his hands deep in his trousers and rocked on his heels observing her. "Return to the ball," he said coldly.

A flicker of uneasiness went through her. Her fingers played nervously with her gloves. Something was dreadfully wrong. He seemed so aloof, so unlike the teasing rogue she had bantered with. "I see. I had wanted to speak with you on an important matter but I will return inside, Your Grace." She offered a small smile. "I look forward to our ride tomorrow, Lucan, perhaps we can speak then."

"No."

She paused and looked back at him, startled.

His expression closed even more. "There will be no more carriage outings, no more dances or opera visits. I thank you for the gracious time you have shown me thus far, Lady Constance."

Her heart slammed into her throat. "I do not understand, I thought we—"

"You thought what? That we were courting?" He inquired in a withering tone.

She could hardly breathe from the emotions tightening her throat. Had he heard some rumor? Since their last kiss at the theatre he had ridden out with her on several more occasions, and they had even stopped at a coffee house yesterday, a thing which had scandalized Charlotte. Why would he be so cold now?

He seemed determined to turn Constance away from him, and she would not stay where she was unwanted. With pride holding her tongue, she swept past him and then hesitated. She walked to him, searching his face. "I feel you when you stare at me, you know. I felt you tonight before I even saw you. That has never happened to me before. Is it the same for you, Lucan?"

"It is dangerous for you to be here in the gardens, Constance. A lady would not have followed me out here."

She stepped closer to him. "Your gaze invited me. I know it, and you know it, Lucan. I *am* a lady, but I have desires too. And I believe in pursuing what I want. Don't you?" He must know what she hinted. She held her breath as she waited for his reply.

"Where is your chaperone?" he all but snarled.

"Charlotte can be marvelously tactful whenever she needs to be."

"You cannot be a lady and a wanton at the same time, Constance. Your eyes beg me to kiss you, to touch you, to take you."

She stared at him fascinated. "Are you saying a lady does not have passion?"

A tick became apparent at his jaw. "A lady's passion is for her husband. Anything that is given or shown to someone to whom you are not married is the surest path to destruction and ruination."

She heard the pain and something darker in his tone. She tried to hold his unwavering stare. It was almost as if he warned her away from him, and she did not understand. The undercurrent of pain in his voice tugged at her. "You speak from experience?"

"I do."

She jerked. "You have ruined someone?"

His mouth was edged with cruelty when he smiled. "No. Someone that I held dear was used, disgraced, and abandoned by someone who claimed to love her."

"Oh my goodness." Constance wanted to ask him who was this person he held dear, but knew he would not disclose such confidence. She noted the flash of pain beneath his cold exterior and wished she was able to draw it all from him. Her decision to leave was thwarted by his revelations. She courted a dangerous situation, but she would not remain long. Even though she now realized she dreamed about a man who had hidden depths she might never be able to reach. "Where is she now?"

"Dead."

He said it so flatly it took her moments for the import of his word to sink in.

Dead? Constance moved closer to him and curled her hand around his arms, hoping to comfort him with her touch. "I am so very sorry, Lucan." Her heart ached as she sensed the smoldering rage beneath his frozen demeanor. "How did she die, if I may be so bold to ask?"

"She was callously used, beaten, and driven to her death," he said bluntly.

Constance stared at him incomprehensibly. She had expected something like a carriage accident or illness. Her eyes roved his face searching for some kind of guide to his thoughts. There was none. His emotionless façade scared her. "Beaten? Driven to her death, as in she killed herself?"

He watched Constance with an intensity that had fear rippling over her skin, and for the first time she became aware of how alone they were in Lady Beaumont's gardens. Constance swallowed, forcing herself not to twitch or shift. She could not explain her sudden unease or the sensations that had her heart jerking. He had always seemed so charming and gentle. "I…"

"Let us not be morbid. This was years ago, Lady Constance."

She felt him retreat, shutting her out. It mattered not that he remained in the same position, her dress curling around his leg in the most intimate fashion. He was no longer present. The teasing suitor she had known this past week had fled, leaving a cold, aloof man. He smiled, and nothing reached his eyes. *What was it?*

She wanted to ask him more of this woman. Who was she? What was her name? Constance had heard no whispers of the Duke of Mondvale having anyone close to him who had killed themselves. It seemed so improbable that the gossip mill would not be buzzing with such information. Though she had not heard he had two younger cousins and an aunt living in Hampshire, either, until he had shared it with her.

He walked over to the small fountain with a cherub spouting water from its mouth. Several stone benches were scattered about, and he sat on one.

Constance sat beside him. "If you ever wish to speak, know I would hold your confidence always."

He stiffened. "Why are you still here, Constance? Why do you behave so recklessly when your reputation already has such a tenuous hold?"

She lifted her chin. "I know you would never hurt me, and no one is paying any attention to me in this crush."

Everything in his face closed down, and her mouth went dry. She shifted closer to him. "What is it?"

The intensity of his stare had a piercing quality that was frightening. "You need to leave and return to the ball. I am sure Lady Ralston is looking for you as we speak."

Anger snapped through Constance and she felt thoroughly provoked. "Why do you push me away? And without any explanation? I know you desire me. You disclose things to me I am sure you share with no other lady. Why don't you speak with my brother about paying addresses to me instead of pushing me away? You must know how I feel about you."

He raked his fingers through his hair in what looked like abject frustration.

"Constance, go inside. I—"

"I believe I am falling in love with you, Lucan."

Shock flittered across his face so fast she wondered if she had imagined it. But what she was certain of was the desire and need that flared in his eyes at her declaration. He felt similarly toward her.

He surged to his feet, staring down at her, his face carefully blank. She rose and stepped close to him, so close that the swell of her breast pressed against him. "I am falling in love with you, Lucan. And I know you have affections for me as well. I would—"

He stole the remainder of her words in a kiss unlike any he had given her before. His lips roamed over hers in a hot, hungry surge of possession, sending waves of sensations through her. His kiss felt desperate and needy. He drew her closer to him, and she lifted onto her toes, responding to his kiss with a dizzying sense of freedom. With a muffled groan, he deepened it and stepped with her so her back rested against the fountain's edge. He pulled his lips from hers, breathing raggedly. He whispered her name rough and gravelly in the dark and she trembled.

"Do not stop kissing me, Lucan," she whispered.

He whispered something she did not hear and then took her mouth in another powerful kiss. She opened her lips to the thrust of his tongue, and pleasure stabbed to her heart. He had never touched her with such fierceness, such passion, and she sank into his embrace, entwining around him like a vine.

His fingers were not idle as they caressed her cheeks, her neck, and slipped down to the mound of her breast. She trembled at his touch. With a gentleness that belied the intensity of how his mouth ravished her, he pulled the buttons to her dress and unlaced her corset as much as he could. He tugged at her gown and revealed her breast to the cool air.

Shock stilled her body as heat flushed her skin. Never had she been this exposed to a man before—and in Lady Beaumont's *garden*! He pulled his lips from Constance's, his head dipping to allow his tongue to lash at her sensitive nipple. He sucked her deep into his mouth, and her body jerked under the burn of pleasure, eroding all rational thought. Her breath caught on a surge of yearning so abrupt and intense it felt like pain.

He released her breast and traced kisses up her neck, nipping at her lips. "Why did you not stay away from me?" he demanded roughly, then pressed another deep kiss on her lips.

She pulled her lips away, confused. "Lucan, I—"

He swallowed her response, his hands kneading her hips. Her desire heightened as he dragged her dress up the length of her legs, conforming her petticoats to his will. He trailed his fingers up the length of her leg, and over her silken stockings. Then he explored farther, letting his hand drift up the sensitive skin of her inner thigh. His long fingers slipped between the juncture of her thighs, parted her drawers, feeling her most intimate spot. It was decadent and wicked.

Oh, God. Constance ripped her mouth from his and pressed her head hard against his shoulder, her face hot with mortification. The clamoring of her heartbeat seemed to drive the air from her lungs, and confusion washed over her, as she tried to assimilate the feelings that throbbed so strangely between her legs.

She swallowed as he slid one long finger slowly into the heart of her, sending a bolt of exquisite sensation through her. Hot, drowning pleasure gripped her as he started a slow glide and retreat. Wetness coated his fingers, and her hips arced into his hands. Moans she could not control ripped from deep inside of her, and Constance bit into his shoulder to prevent herself from crying out, as her stomach tightened in painful need.

"You are so responsive." The dark velvet rasp of his voice sank into her, promising unimaginable pleasures.

He pressed his leg between hers and shifted his foot widening her more to his intimate caress. Her cry was choked off as his fingers pressed deeper.

"Kiss me, my sweet," he murmured roughly and she complied.

She whimpered in his mouth and flinched as a second finger probed at her entrance. She stiffened, and he caressed her until his thumb pressed against a spot that had her arcing into him, her mind hazy from need. The bite of pain at the entry of his two fingers were drowned out under the exquisite sensation that splintered her body.

His lips gentled, and her body trembled in the aftermath of such vicious pleasure. He gently eased his fingers from her body, and licked her wetness from them. Her gaze fixated on his mouth as his tongue flicked over his fingers and shocking arousal burned in her veins at his action. He then dipped his head, peppering soothing kisses along her lips and jawline.

Constance trembled and a deep fear filled her. He embodied every secret fantasy she had ever had. She was more like her mother than she realized for he did not speak of marriage, yet she was allowing such liberties. *I* am *a wanton.*

With a harsh groan he pulled away from her, and with swift efficiency, he re-laced her corset and fixed her gown. "Please forgive me for losing control, Constance. Tidy your hair. I will do my utmost best to see that you are returned inside without being seen."

She nodded, uncertain how to proceed after such startling intimacy. "Shall I expect you tomorrow?"

He froze. "I will not be calling on you again."

"Why?" she asked bluntly.

His eyes narrowed. "Leave before I bend you over and fuck you here."

She stumbled back and stared at him with widened eyes. She searched his gaze, trying to understand why he was being so vulgar. Their entire encounter had been magical. She may not know the word, but his tone said everything. "Why do you push me away with such crude words?"

He tensed.

"Do you think me so foolish I would not see, Lucan?"

He jerked from her, raking his hand though his hair.

She blinked bemused at the red stain that heightened his stunning cheekbones. She suddenly realized he was not all that comfortable with how he spoke to her. "Are you blushing, Lucan?"

His look of male affront had her smiling, dispelling some of her unease.

"If you do not leave now, I am going to lay you down and take my pleasure with you. Is that what you want?"

"Absolutely not." She stepped back warily, her heart pounding.

"Are you so sure, Lady Constance? Your continued presence indicates you *want* me to toss up your skirts." His words were cutting like a knife.

"You are being deliberately hurtful, and I see you are pushing me from you. I only want to know why, so I will not be haunted by it," she whispered hoarsely.

"I push you away for your own good."

"My own good?" she parroted, feeling terrified by his distance.

Lucan hissed out a frustrated breath "I want more…I want to be inside you. If you do not step away from me I will lose control and take you in the gardens. I want to be in your heat and wetness so bad I dream of it. And by pushing you away that is what I prevent, for it would surely ruin you. But is it that you want me to take you *now*?"

The blood drained from her face. "No!" she muttered horrified at his blatant suggestions. Yet she was intrigued by his need. She stepped farther away, but he advanced on her and his hands spanned her waist as he lifted her. He lowered her so she straddled his knee and she could feel every muscle of his thigh straight to her core.

"I can see that you burn for me, Constance, and it is so damn tempting. Even now I can feel your heat, your desire. You yearn to know how it feels to have a man between your legs riding you. And not just any man, *me*, taking you, pleasuring you, teaching you passion." He pressed a hard kiss to her lips, the apparent need on his face searing her. "I know this, for *every night* you torment me with dreams of how you would feel sheathed on my cock. I fantasize what it would be like to walk beside you, laugh with you, to have children with you."

Shock held her still. "I…" No one had ever looked at her like Lucan, touched her as he did. She had been always sheltered, protected, pampered by her brothers and everyone in her life. *Sheathed on his cock?* She could only imagine what he meant. He shifted his thigh, rubbing against her core, and fire shot through her body scandalizing her. But the greater thing that enthralled her was what he had said. Wild hope surged inside of her. "Children, Lucan?"

She saw the utter shock that filled his eyes before his expression grew impassive. He lowered her to her feet and withdrew.

She knew that was what he uttered. "You said children, Lucan. What are you saying?" She tried to keep the hope out of her voice.

He raked his hands through his hair with an angry curse. "I did not mean to say that," he growled.

"Don't be a coward," she said, not retreating. "You obviously want me as much as I want you. And you said *children*. I do desire your kisses, and I do want to explore this hunger that rages between us, which springs to life from a glance, a fleeting kiss. I want to walk and laugh with you as well. I also see the possibilities of us together, having such a life together, growing to love and cherish each other."

He closed his eyes as if pained. "I hope one day you will forgive me."

She stared into his eyes in puzzlement. Forgiveness for what? "What is it, Lucan?"

He drew her close and pressed a gentle kiss along her forehead. Confusion churned in her. She could feel the regret in his touch.

"Good-bye, Constance."

The remoteness she saw in his expression scared her. She gripped his hand, preventing him from moving away. "I am confused, Lucan, I—"

He gently removed her grip. "Let me be as clear as I can. I made an error in pursuing you. I am no longer interested in riding out with you, and this will be the last you will see of me."

"I thought you would speak to my brother and—"

"You thought wrong," he said flatly.

The pain knifing through Constance almost drove her to her knees. She stared into his dark sensual features, searching for a hint of the sweet, tender lover she'd been falling for.

"You were just kissing me…touching me… I—"

His low mocking chuckle vibrated through her and tears burned her eyes.

"That was nothing special, an everyday occurrence between a man and a woman. Disabuse yourself of the notion that it meant something more."

A sickening sensation entered her stomach, and she felt faint. Her hands shook, and she took deep breaths to prevent herself from throwing up. "I don't understand." *Oh, God.* "Is it because I am a bastard?" She was proud that her voice did not shake.

The distance in his eyes had pain clawing at her throat. She desperately wanted to leave, to weep her anguish in private. How could he be so cruel? She was ashamed of the tears that splashed onto her cheeks, and even more so from the words that escaped her lips. "I am in love with you, Lucan, and I know you feel something for me, something deeper than friendship, so I cannot understand why you are being so distant. Please confide in me."

"Good-bye, Lady Constance." Then he turned and walked away.

She could not comprehend his coldness after all they had shared. Constance felt hollow, like some vital part of her had been crushed, but she did not want him to see how badly he had shattered her. She wanted to travel home right away, curl up in a ball, and weep, curse, and howl. And even then, the pain would not lessen. She touched him out of need and desire, allowed him so much more because she was falling in love with him. Every touch, every kiss, and every groan she pulled from him had been nothing special to Lucan. Existence had never seemed so devoid of life.

Chapter Ten

A fire in the brazier warmed the parlor in Lucan's apartments, but its heat did not reach him. He felt cold and empty. For the first time since he'd taken on his path to end Calydon, Lucan felt a deep wash of regret. He had convinced himself over the long months of plotting, his revenge would be sweet when he ruined Constance in the same way Calydon had done Marissa. Instead, its taste was bitter and vile, and Lucan had not even executed his plan.

It had been his full intention to have them discovered in a compromising position and to then refuse to marry her. Her ruination would have been completed. But he had been unable to do it. He had decided to find another path to bring down Calydon. But, God, the look in Constance's eyes.

I feel you when you stare at me, you know. I felt you tonight before I even saw you. That has never happened to me before. Is it the same for you, Lucan?

When she had asked Lucan that, he had wanted to

howl "yes". He'd remained silent, fearing if he answered, she would see the truth. The instant her gaze touched him, it was as if some unseen force burned him, bespelled him, and he only had to quickly scan the crowd to find her stare hot with need caressing him.

He was aware of a strange numbness somewhere deep inside himself. After what had happened to Marissa he had promised himself he would never bed an innocent, never entangle himself with one. He had shattered the dreams and hopes he saw in Constance's eyes. He supposed every young girl dreamed of courtship and marriage. It had been clear she expected him to declare for her. It made him feel hollow to think he had planned on doing worse to her. And for what? He doubted Calydon could feel the pain Lucan had felt when he learned he had lost Marissa so cruelly.

Please confide in me.

The memory of the heartfelt plea tormented him, and the knowledge of how much he had hurt Constance cut into him like a knife. He could hardly explain that he had been trying to save her from himself. The huge pool of pain that had reflected in her green eyes had shredded something inside of him.

His sister had been brutally beaten for months, then hung herself. At least Calydon still had Constance. At least Lucan had not executed his vengeance on her. But he could find no comfort in his reasoning.

"Tell me what happened?" Ainsley prompted for the second time from his spot near the mantel.

Lucan did not look at him. Instead he went to the cabinet in his office and poured himself a glass of scotch. He downed the liquor in one swallow and poured another. The door opened and closed quietly, but he did not look up. It would be the Reverend.

"What the hell is going on? Did someone die?"

Lucan lifted his head, surprised to see the club's accountant, his friend Marcus Stone entering. He was their fourth partner in the club. The man took in the wrecked office, the shattered glass, and overturned chairs with cool aplomb, saying nothing at Lucan's apparent loss of control.

"Should I leave and come back?"

Before Lucan could answer him, the Reverend entered, scanned the destruction and poured himself a drink. They all waited on Lucan, his friends, the only ones he had trusted with his plans of vengeance.

"I failed in executing my plan to compromise Lady Constance last night at Lady Beaumont's ball. In order to prevent her from further designs by me I pushed her away with cruel words."

Marcus righted one of the overturned chairs and sat. Lucan could see the puzzlement in his friend's blue eyes. "I don't understand. Isn't that what you wanted? The chit's ruination? Why would you change your course?"

Lucan walked to the east windows that overlooked St. James Park. He dropped his forehead on the cool panes of the glass. He wanted Calydon to pay, but it was Constance enduring the most hurt now.

"I struggled against it, tried to push her away and find another path. When I told her that what has been burgeoning between us meant nothing I...I had not expected the evidence of her anguish to affect me so. There is a pain in my chest, a torment in my mind that will not ease."

There was a pregnant silence.

"I have never seen you wax poetic over any female before," the Reverend said, moving to stand beside him. "If you have such feelings for Lady Constance why not simply marry her? You are now a duke, I expect marriage to be somewhere in your future with your responsibilities to the title."

"I cannot."

"You can do anything you wish, Lucan," the Reverend countered.

Lucan straightened, closing himself off from all the feelings ravaging inside. "I will not marry into the family of the man that helped to destroy my sister. I will not forgive Calydon, and I will not halt my destruction of him. I shall direct my actions so that Constance is not adversely affected."

The Reverend sighed. "Marcus has uncovered the other interests Calydon has invested in and who owns the majority. There are several that are in debt to us and can be manipulated."

Lucan walked over to the table, where his friends showed him reports of holdings and schemes many did not know Calydon owned or was involved in. Lucan wanted to know everything about the reclusive duke. He would not rest until he completed his revenge. Only his vow felt hollow, his heart too shredded to be invested deeply. Constance would haunt him for months. The memory of her taste on his tongue, her hot moans, her eagerness, and the tight clasp that had nearly choked his fingers. Hell. *You could have her forever*, an insidious voice whispered. Her passion, her laughter, the hope, the future in her gaze.

He slammed the shutters down, and directed his attention to the conversation around the table. A few minutes later, his friends departed, and he availed himself to all the liquor in the cabinet. For the first time in years, he got roaring drunk.

There was no sense of triumph that he had hurt Constance at all, only shame that he had sought to destroy someone so refreshingly pure and beautiful.

For a sin that was not hers.

• • •

Dressed in her light blue morning tea gown, Constance sat in the chair near the window in the drawing room and gazed out into the gardens. The late afternoon sun streamed through the windows, but it did not bring the warmth she expected. She doubted anything could thaw her. It had been a week since she'd last seen Lucan, and she was still not at peace.

She could not seem to sort out the conflicted emotions bubbling inside her with such viciousness. She raged at him, hating him with such passion she trembled. Then it would switch so fast to deep yearning, tears would come to her eyes. She resented both feelings. She preferred to dwell where there was no pain, only coldness.

I fantasize what it would be like to walk beside you, laugh with you, to have children with you. How could he have said such words and then walked away? The notion that she had been wrong about him all this time was too staggering to contemplate or accept.

A spasm of anguish snaked through her. She had trusted him. How naive she had been. But it was her own foolish daring and desires that made for such an outcome to be possible. She could not shy from that, no matter how painful the acknowledgement was. She now believed Lucan was as wickedly unprincipled as society said, despite being the only man to ever make her heart stutter. She only had to think his name, and the memory of his taste, the feel of his lips on hers, on her breast, and the feel of his fingers between her thighs would spiral heat wicked and hot through her. She was confounded by it. He had devastated her and she still thought about their kisses, about the pleasures he had bestowed on her.

She had always dreamed about romance, a dashing prince charming sweeping her off her feet with dances and picnics, strolls by the waterfront and stolen kisses. Constance wanted love, family, laughter, a togetherness that had been missing from her childhood. She had felt foolish hope that her illegitimacy would not deter a suitor. After all, she was wealthy, and she was without illusions about her beauty. It was hard to credit that it was her bastardy that drove him away. He had known before he called upon her. What had changed his mind? The strolls by the water fronts, the picnics and outings could not have been in vain on his part. Something had happened, and she needed to know what. She could deny no more that unless she knew, it would forever haunt her.

The day passed in a grim kind of blur as she made her plans. Only Charlotte seemed to pick up on Constance's despondency. Charlotte had been outraged when Constance explained all that happened. She had seen the looks of concern from her mother and father, and had been grateful they had not probed.

The evening dinner was a quiet, informal affair. She lingered for what seemed an appropriate amount of time that would not rouse concern, before she excused herself. An hour later, she felt as if she had walked a hole into the carpet in her chamber.

She vacillated between talking herself into seeing Lucan and demanding answers, and berating herself for even thinking of being so bold, so reckless. She had been too shocked at Lady Beaumont's ball to demand he give her an appropriate answer. He had not officially declared his intention to her family, but she refused to accept that his attentions had meant nothing. With that firm thought, she launched into motion.

She rang for a bath and ordered a gown to be readied. She knew it would take a while but she did not care. She *would* see him tonight. She asked her maid to be circumspect and Constance could see the concern in Anne's eyes. It was not hard for Constance to keep the anger alive while she completed her *toilette*. She did not even flinch when her corset was drawn tighter than necessary. Nothing would dissuade her from her path.

She was not surprised when an hour later, Charlotte knocked on the door while the finishing touches were being placed to her hair. Charlotte drew in a startled breath when she noticed the black domino cape laid out on the bed, along with Constance's golden masquerade mask. "Constance, have you lost your marbles?" Charlotte hissed.

Constance waved her hands, dismissing Anne, and rose from in front of the vanity to face Charlotte.

"No, I have not," Constance said brusquely.

"Where are you headed? Lord and Lady Radcliffe have retired for the night. So who are you heading out with and to *where*?"

Constance ignored Charlotte's strident demand and took up the cape. "Help me."

"Constance," Charlotte snapped in exasperation. She helped Constance into her cape and Constance turned to the mirror and slipped on her mask.

With the wig borrowed from her mother's chamber covering her golden hair, she was not recognizable. She took a deep breath and turned to face Charlotte. "I made this decision two days ago, but I am just finding the courage to act on it, Charlotte. I must see Luca—the duke or I will forever live with this wealth of doubt, pain, and anger inside. I doubt you will understand, but that is all right. I expect no one will understand what I am feeling. But I do ask you to keep my confidence."

"You cannot head to his residence alone," Charlotte breathed in shock. "You court complete ruination."

Constance frowned. "I am already ruined in society's eyes, and I will not let my actions be dictated by them. Besides, you are forgetting I am in masquerade."

The silence in the chamber was pronounced.

"Connie…"

"I will be fine, Char. Mother and father are sleeping, and I will be going through the back entrance. When I made the decision to leave, I ordered the carriage to be ready. I have also ensured the crest will be covered. Do not wait up for me. I will be back in a few hours."

"I think not. I am coming with you."

"Char—"

Charlotte raised her hand to halt Constance's speech. "That is the only way I am letting you out of here without raising a ruckus. Allow me to get my domino and mask, and we will be off."

"I am heading to his club, not his town house," Constance

confessed.

"I suspected as much," Charlotte replied, before sweeping out of the chamber.

Constance felt a deep sense of relief curling through her. Though she had been sure of what she had to do, she had felt trepidation about her chosen path. The support of Charlotte meant everything, and Constance would tell her so.

The clock struck midnight as they crept down the back stairs, careful to be quiet. They exited to the back gardens and walked with swift steps to where the carriage waited. Her heart thundered, and she prayed she was not making another foolish decision as Charlotte feared. A decision that would complete the breaking of Constance's heart. But she needed to understand. If only to rout Lucan from her heart, a place she feared he had already been deeply embedded.

Chapter Eleven

Constance walked up to the most luxurious gaming club in all of London as if it were a normal occurrence to do so and knocked. A man who seemed to be the majordomo opened the door. He was dressed in a black evening coat, snowy white undershirt, and white bow tie, with his hair slicked back without a strand out of place. He would have looked elegant and dashing if not for the cold, hard expression on his face.

He raised a brow and ran an insolent gaze over her length. His regard switched to Charlotte and a quick frown chased his features.

"I... We..." Constance bit her lips hard wondering if she should simply say the secret word.

"Your rings?" he asked in a silted voice, his question encompassing her and Charlotte.

Constance swallowed and prayed Lucan had not been jesting. "Revenant."

The man stiffened, peered at her for a few long seconds,

and then sketched a deep bow. "Lord Ainsley, at your service. This way ladies," he said after taking their coats and dominos and handing it to another man.

The Earl of Ainsley? She wanted to question why he had been the one to open the club door, but she kept her nose firmly to herself. He prowled ahead of them at a leisurely pace. Charlotte adjusted her mask and glanced at Constance. She lifted her chin and walked after the man. They traveled through a long hall, passed several doors, and Constance could hear the din of laughter filtering to the hall. They came upon a massive door, which swung open without the man even knocking. He waved them through, and Constance stepped into the sheer opulence of a grand ballroom. She grounded to a halt and Charlotte almost ran into her.

Three floors rose in stunning splendor. The ceiling was made of stained-glass panels and dozens of glittering chandeliers hung suspended, their lights dancing off the hundreds of men and women in their finery. The masks of the patrons glittered, some fanciful, some exquisitely designed, and some darkly fashioned into looks of darkness and decadence. Couples embraced publicly in several corners on chaise lounges, and those who danced were certainly closer than what was appropriate. Constance swallowed as she saw a man and woman kissing in the most scandalous fashion for all to see. She became painfully aware how much young ladies of society were sheltered. Suddenly her corset felt too tight and fear wafted through her. She was out of her league.

But she had to admit the place was magnificent. The décor consisted of dark, rich paneled woods, peach and silver velvet drapes lined the walls, and the luxurious orient carpet that covered the floors and the staircase was the richest and most beautiful she had ever seen. The walls were lined with massive gilded columns that were swathed in cloths with oriental colors so vibrant they seemed exotic. Raucous laughter and conversation spilled down the stairs and Constance stared in awe at the dozens of glasses layered on each other in a fountain floating with golden liquid.

"What is it?"

"Champagne," the earl responded.

A fountain of champagne? The very notion was simply… *decadent*. "Is this why Mondvale is referred to as the Lord of Sin?" the question spilled out before she could stop herself.

Lord Ainsley glanced at her almost bemusedly. "If you are asking me if Lucan's moniker was given because he dazzled society with a fountain of champagne you should not be here, Lady Constance. You are ignorant of what is considered sinful."

Charlotte gasped and Constance froze. How did he know it was her? "I…"

A fleeting smile touched his lips. "Relax, your secret is safe with me. I will have someone attend to you."

Before she could speak, he melted away into the crowd.

"Oh my goodness, Connie, he knew who you were. I think we need to leave immediately."

"He said we were safe."

Charlotte gaped at her. "And you believed *him*?"

A loud shriek drew Constance's gaze to a lady slapping a man kissing the globes of her breasts. Constance remembered Lucan had said he catered to Society's finest. The stunning hypocrisy of everything had a surge of rage firing in her veins. Here they chortled, tossed the dice, danced the most scandalous dances, and they were members of the *haute monde*. But they felt protected behind their masks. Actions they would judge other people for, cut them for, refused to speak with them for, they were here indulging in liberally. *The hypocrites*.

A man appeared at their side as if by magic with two glasses of champagne. "What will be your pleasures this evening, madams? The dancers will soon be out in the smaller ballroom if you would like to observe. We have several card parties tonight. Games of Baccarat, poker, Hazard, roulette, Vingt et un, and Faro running in the game rooms, or if you would like to have dinner—"

"I would like to see the Duke of Mondvale," she interrupted him curtly.

"Very well, this way, Madame."

They walked around the crush of people to a slim foyer that ran almost parallel to the ballroom. Constance could not help ogling the magnificence of the place. They entered what appeared to be the smaller ballroom, and she slowly blinked. Everyone there was dressed in elaborate costumes and wore masks. It had been a stab in the dark on her part to appear incognito. Never had it occurred to her that everyone else would be similarly attired.

He led them to a chaise near the refreshment table. "I will inform His Grace you are here."

"Thank you."

"Whom may I tell His Grace is requesting his presence?"

She inhaled to steady her nerves. "Please inform him that Miss Desiree Hastings is here, and will not leave until she has an audience."

He sketched another small bow and melted away.

Constance was surprised at how quiet the crowd was

as if they waited for something to start. She strained to see where they were all looking. The crowd then roared in approval and her lips parted in astonishment as scantily dressed women twirled out in perfect synchronization onto a space made for them on the ballroom floor.

"My goodness!" Charlotte exclaimed.

Constance thought they were beautiful as they launched into a vigorous dance, their legs kicking scandalously high in such perfect unison. With an unwilling fascination she could not control, she rose to her feet and strolled closer for a better view. Her breath caught. She could see the ladies garters, black stockings, and drawers as they kicked and twirled their long red shirts. She gasped as the dancers struck several provocative poses and then bent over, throwing their skirts over their backs, showing their rear end to the cheering audience.

She was certainly standing in a den of sin and decadence, and she was about to have a private audience with the man who lorded over it.

She was definitely out of her element.

• • •

Lucan still could not credit that Constance was in his club. When Thomas had informed Lucan that a Miss Desiree Hastings was here to see him he had stuttered. His factotum in turn had been intrigued that a woman had rendered Lucan to such a state.

Not even a few seconds had passed when Ainsley strolled into the office.

"Lady Constance—"

"Thomas informed me," Lucan snapped.

Ainsley smiled. "You need to get down there soon. The lady is oblivious, but I have seen more than a few curious looks aimed her way, hungry looks," he drawled.

Ignoring him, Lucan left his office with the firm intention of escorting her away from the premises.

"I have told Thomas to escort her to the smaller ball-room," Ainsley said behind him, laughter rife in his tone.

Their private apartments and offices were on the third floor of the building, so it would take Lucan a few minutes to reach her. Thrusting his hands in his pockets, he forced himself to walk down the halls at a measured pace. It would not do for anyone to see him running, especially one of his interfering friends.

He descended to the second floor and walked along the hallway to the door leading to the smaller ballroom. He entered and scanned the crowd from the balcony looking for her unique blond hair. The reckless fool probably did not even realize how recognizable she was. The highest echelons of society were members of *Decadence*. All of his patrons were gentry mixed with the *haute monde*. She could be recognized by anyone.

The idea of her being at the club rattled him. Whatever distance he placed between them while he plotted to bring down Calydon was necessary. For Constance made him yearn for the impossible, to put aside his vengeance and pursue a life with her. She was proving to be his most dangerous opponent yet. No other had ever made him doubt his chosen path as she did now. Not even his closest friends had the power to sway him with their arguments. But she had the capability to do so with a mere stare. And she was *here*.

Lucan stood transfixed when he identified her. She wore an icy blue gown cut to showcase her exquisite charms. He would recognize her shape anywhere, the sharp but feminine shape of her face, and sensually curved lips. She had been ingenious enough to don a vivid red wig that complemented her creamy skin tone in the most alluring manner. The eye mask she also wore served to disguise her even further. If he had not been intimately acquainted with her, he would not have known he was looking at Lady Constance. Not so foolish after all, but still reckless.

A slow appreciative whistle came from his left, and Marcus came up beside him. Lucan gritted his teeth in annoyance for his friend seemed as equally transfixed.

"Who is she?"

"Out of bounds," Lucan said flatly. He could feel Marcus's astonishment. It was unlike Lucan to be possessive of any female.

Marcus' gaze slashed back to her. "My God, is that Lady Constance? I have heard about her charms from Ainsley and the Reverend, but I thought they exaggerated."

At Lucan's silence Marcus chuckled. "It is, isn't it? I had heard the lady to be blond. But from the way your hands are digging into the railings—"

"It is her," Lucan said cutting off Marcus' taunting.

Lucan forcibly relaxed his hand and released the balcony railing.

"Fearless little thing isn't she?"

"I think you mean reckless," Lucan growled.

Marcus glanced at him in apparent bemusement. "I think her presence here tonight is all you need to draw Calydon into a deeper trap of your making. Yet you seem angry with her." He continued in his taunting drawl, "Curious indeed.

I am beginning to think the Reverend is correct in his assertions. You need to marry the lady."

Lucan narrowed his gaze, taking in her fascination with the women dancing the can-can. Someone moved to stand beside her, and he recognized Lady Ralston from her posture alone. Both of them were oblivious to the various stares directed their way. All from men, and from the hunger in their regard, he knew without a doubt what they were thinking.

"Damn it!" he was thoroughly annoyed with both women. The risk they took amazed him.

"And who is that?" Marcus asked. His gazed directed solely on Constance's companion.

"Lady Ralston."

"Is she off bounds as well?"

"No, but tread carefully. The lady is too fragile for your attentions. I can assure you she is not here for any dalliance."

Marcus frowned. "Fragile?"

"Her husband was not the most pleasant fellow."

Marcus stiffened. "I forgot you have a dossier on almost everyone in contact with Lady Constance. So the lady is married."

Lucan threw a curious look at Marcus. He sounded disappointed. Too disappointed. Lady Ralston was a fetching young lady. Her dark hair was cropped into short riotous curls, and without a mane of hair distracting an observer, one could easily immerse themselves in the prettiness of her pixie features. But it was her turquoise eyes that were her most stunning feature.

"Widowed," Lucan imparted. "She married at seventeen to the Earl of Ralston and was widowed two years later. It has been two years since he passed, and the lady has not shown favor to anyone. She has been hounded by a few to become their mistress, a notable attempt was made by the Viscount of Morley, but the lady declined all offers. Instead she chose to work as a ladies companion, despite the amount of debt the late earl left."

"What are you going to do in relation to Lady Constance? It is evident the lady did not agree with whatever you said to her in the gardens," Marcus said after a few quiet moments.

"It seems I need to be more brutal," Lucan mused.

Without waiting for Marcus's reply, Lucan descended the stairs and headed toward Constance. He did not trust the curl of anticipation that traveled inside of him. He hoped he had the strength to turn her away and not succumb to the raging lust that leapt to life inside of him the moment he had been told she was in his club. If he took her, he would ruin her further when he now wanted her protected. For though the Reverend and Ainsley encouraged him, he would never marry her, no matter how tempting the thought.

Chapter Twelve

Constance felt Lucan before she saw him. She glanced up and spied him prowling toward her. He was exquisitely dressed in black trousers and a pristine white shirt that emphasized the broad width of his shoulders, and a black tailcoat cut to fit his frame superbly. The only dash of color was his dark toned silver waistcoat. She guarded herself against the pleasure tingling through her. The man who walked toward her was coolly distant, and no sign of welcome or even pleasure at seeing her showed on his face.

"Why are you here?" he demanded upon reaching her.

She bit back her instinctive angry retort. "I would like to see you in private," she said firmly. "I risked much to speak with you, and I would welcome an audience with you."

His eyes hardened, and she tried not to fidget. She must appear resolute and unflappable.

"Welcome to *Decadence*, Miss Hastings, I am Marcus Stone. Please allow me to entertain your companion while you confer with His Grace in private," the man who had walked up beside Lucan drawled smoothly. Mr. Stone was a handsome sort, but in a rough way. His dark brown hair was long enough to be tied in a queue, and his pale blue eyes seemed to laugh at her.

Lucan's lips flattened and the glare he directed at Mr. Stone shriveled her inside, even though it was not aimed at her. Mr. Stone only smiled and held his arm out to Charlotte. Constance heard Charlotte's soft indrawn breath, but she laid her hand on his sleeve. Constance glanced at Charlotte and was surprised to see a blush on her cheeks.

"I…thank you, Mr. Stone," Constance replied, unsure of what else to say.

He inclined his head and walked away with Charlotte, who looked over her shoulder and mouthed for Constance to be careful. Constance nodded in confirmation and gave her a reassuring smile.

She glanced at Lucan to see him watching Mr. Stone and Charlotte with a neutral mien.

"Will she be safe with Mr. Stone?"

Cold silver eyes looked down on her. "Lady Ralston is a widow. I am sure she knew what Mr. Stone wanted when he led her away."

She gaped at him. "Are you saying he has designs on Charlotte?" Constance squeaked, wondering if that was what she had seen on the man's face while he looked at her friend. His regard had been unsettling.

"She is in capable hands," he said flatly.

Constance considered his closed expression for a few seconds. "Will we go somewhere to converse?"

He stared at her for the longest while without responding

and nervousness shivered inside of her.

"Follow me," he clipped.

She released the pent up breath she had been holding and walked beside him. It had been a gamble that he would accede to her demand. She had fully expected him to put up a greater fight and possibly drag her outside to her waiting carriage. Without speaking, he ascended the stairs that led from the room. After climbing a second flight of carpeted stairs, the din of everything droned away, and she could hear nothing from the hallway along which they walked. Then he opened an oak door and she entered what looked like a library.

"Do you understand how dangerous it is for you to be here?" he asked as they entered.

"To my reputation?"

"Yes."

"I doubt I am in danger of being recognized. I was very discreet."

She held her breath at the look he leveled on her. He arched his brow insolently and glanced around the library, driving home how secluded they were and that she had deliberately snuck out to be at his club. Her cheeks flamed.

He rang a bell and a butler showed up as if he had been stationed at the door.

"Bring the carriage around for the lady. She will be leaving shortly."

She waited until the butler closed the door. "I am not leaving," she said firmly. "Not until you explain to me in full why you decided to end our friendship."

"I was not aware we were friends."

"You know what I mean, Lucan." Constance moved

and perched on the side of the sofa, her entire attention on him. "I deserve to know what happened. What you think warranted treating me with such disregard. I have been in a torment of doubt wondering why you decided to halt your courtship. I refuse to be that person where I do not ask for answers, but speculate in misery."

"I was never courting you."

She slowly stood from her perch. "I know you never declared to my family but—"

Her words tapered off as he walked over to her, and from the look on his face she knew she would not like what he was about to say.

"I only got close to you so I could use you against Calydon."

She was sure she misheard. "I beg your pardon?"

"Calydon ruined my sister, and I thought it apt to ruin his in return. That was all, Constance."

There was a loud buzzing in her head as she tried to comprehend. Lucan had only been using her? To hurt Sebastian? Her mind latched onto possibly the safest topic so she would not lose control. "You have a sister?"

"Had."

Someone that I held dear was used, disgraced, and abandoned by someone who claimed to love her.

Constance stepped around him, her hands clasped together to prevent their shaking. She spun to see he had turned with her, watching her with an expression of indifference. "Your sister was the one you held dear to you…that died?"

She saw the answer in his eyes. Some raw and powerful emotion flashed in his silver gaze before the shutters came down.

She nodded weakly. "I see. And everything between us,

our carriage rides, picnic, kisses and…" — she flushed — "you were just using me?" He had wanted to ruin her as Sebastian had ruined his sister. *Good heavens!* She pressed a fist to her stomach, suddenly unsure if she wanted the answer. "Tell me about your sister, please, Lucan. I know Sebastian would never hurt anyone intentionally."

"No," Lucan growled, anger leaping to his face. "My sister will never be up for discussion. You wanted answers as to why I am not interested in you. You have it." He stalked over to Constance, and she took a wary step backward. Her back pressed against the bookcase, and she lifted her chin as he stopped so close she felt the heat of him.

"My interest in you was only to use you to hurt Calydon, nothing more. I had intended for you to be seen with me at Lady Beaumont's ball in a compromising position."

Her heart stopped beating.

He visibly gritted his teeth. "But I could not do it. I realized, albeit a little late, that Calydon's sin was not yours to bear. But it seems I may still get my wish, for you are here, behaving with reckless disregard for your tenuous position in society!"

Lucan had planned on compromising her? She felt mortified. She had really believed he had been courting her, that he was falling in love with her. But it had all been about lowering her defenses, leading her to ruin. A cold chill washed over her. "You never intended to court me, to offer for me?" Constance asked in a suffocated voice.

"No," he said softly. "I have no intention of marrying you or any other society miss."

"Then why did you kiss me, touch me?"

"You made it appallingly easy to be seduced, Lady

Constance."

The pain clawing at Constance's throat burned away under the rush of rage, and her hand flew as if by its own volition to slap him. With a quick reflex that startled her, he captured her hand in a gentle hold.

"Constance—"

"Don't speak my name," she breathed. "I suppose you think because you did not compromise me you were acting honorably? Well let me tell you, Your Grace, you are a coward," she choked out. "I do not believe the passion and time we shared was all to ruin me. That could have been achieved without our rides and many outings. I know why you chose to pull away, but you are such a damn coward you prefer to hurt me for a vengeance you do not wish to explain. I *see* how you watch me, how you smile when I laugh. I feel your hunger for me, and I even know when you are aroused and trying to hide it. I hope your vengeance will keep you warm and satisfied for years to come. I will see myself out."

She wrenched away from him and stormed toward the door. She gasped as hands spanned her waist from behind and lifted her. He tumbled with her onto the sofa, twisting so that he took the brunt of their fall. She landed with an *oomph* on his chest and before she could protest, he pulled her to him and took her mouth in a carnal kiss. The sudden shift from anger to desire was a shock to her system. His tongue plunged past her lips, wicked and alluring. The lush eroticism of his actions made her tremble, and she became helpless against his kiss, a kiss that was ruthless in its demand. His lips stroked over hers, his tongue flickering deep inside.

A craving for him stormed through her defenses, and she fisted her hands in his hair and returned his kiss with all her pent up anger and desire. There was a rustle of silk as he slid her dress up, bunching her mass of petticoats around her thighs. She gasped into his mouth as his fingers unerringly found her slick entrance through the slit in her drawers. Without breaking their embrace, he inserted a finger inside of her, the stroke of his finger matching his tongue, deep and sensual. Constance felt as if fire itself lighted in her veins. Sensations raced across her skin, tightening pleasures low between her legs. She moaned and arched her hip as he inserted a second digit. Despite the burn, the stretch, and the ache, she wanted more. He stroked somewhere deep inside that shot a bolt of pleasure up to her breasts. They felt heavy, and she desperately wanted them free of the corset. He pulled his lips from hers, trailing kisses along her neck to the globes of her breast, but never letting up on the wicked caress between her legs. She let out a hoarse cry as a heavy tide of ecstasy swept over her, splintering her senses.

"So damn beautiful," he muttered roughly.

He slid from the sofa so that he knelt in front of her and removed his spectacles, placing them beside her on the sofa. He pushed her dress farther up to her hips, and tugged off her drawers baring her to his gaze. A frisson of dangerous exhilaration gripped her, and acting on an instinct she had not known she possessed, she widened her thighs more for him. Emotions she was not able to name flared in the depth of his eyes as he watched her splayed before him so scandalously. Without saying anything, he dipped his head and kissed her in a place she never dreamed could be kissed.

"I don't think this is proper, Lucan," she protested, rather too weakly.

Instinctively Constance slid her hands through his thick

hair, and she did not know if she wanted to push him away or pull his head more firmly against her. His tongue curled and dipped, before his teeth gently clamped over her knot of pleasure with scorching precision. *Definitely hold his head more firmly*, she reasoned hazily as delight pulsed through her. She shivered violently when the sensual glide of his tongue took her to the same edge his fingers had earlier. But it felt different, gentle and sweeter, but somehow more powerful. The sensations that roared through her had her back bowing off the sofa and uncontrolled cries spilling from her lips as her body surrendered.

Her body felt languid and unfamiliar as it came down from the stunning pleasures. Lucan slowly lowered her dress and petticoats, resting his forehead against her quivering stomach. Minutes passed in silence, and he remained kneeled before her, head rested against her, not speaking or moving.

She knew without a doubt whatever he said next would determine the course of her future with him. She could feel him thinking, fighting with whatever demons were pushing him away from her. Her heart went calm and she simply waited until he was ready, hoping he would confide in her about his sister and whatever he thought Sebastian had done. The intimacy of the moment did not escape her, and it somehow felt more intimate than the pleasure he had just bestowed upon her. A log rolled in the fireplace, and his fingers tightened against her hips. He pressed the softest of kiss against her stomach and then lifted his head. Her heart slammed into her throat. His features were set in dark foreboding lines.

"I do feel something fierce for you, and I would be more than a coward to not admit it. I want to be with you when you are not here. I look for your smiles in the simplest of actions. Am I falling in love? I do not know… I only know there are times I hunger for your presence if only to converse. I desire you more each time I see you. But your brother is my enemy, and that will never change. He ruined my sister, hurt her unimaginably, and then abandoned her. I cannot see you again, Lady Constance, nor will you be admitted to *Decadence* again for you make me doubt my path, and it is a path I will not be swayed from."

Pain sliced through her, but she was careful not to show her emotions. The man that touched her with such passion, introduced her to pleasure, was a man that wanted her, *needed* her even, and she would concentrate on those feelings. She shifted onto the sofa, shimmying lower so she slid against his chest until she kneeled with him. Leaning back and tilting her head, she held his gaze, and surprise flared through his at her actions.

"Tell me that you can bear the thought of *never* speaking with me or kissing me again, and I will walk away and leave you with your vengeance."

His throat convulsed, but he did not speak. Her pulse fluttered wildly when he dropped his forehead to hers and closed his eyes. He shifted, kissed her hair, and Constance smiled. He could not say it. She understood, for he was firmly rooted in her heart and the thought of not exploring the growing need between them was unbearable.

"I can see you are not ready to tell me of your sister. I hope one day I will have your trust and you will unburden to me, Lucan," she whispered. He stiffened, but she continued. "I know Sebastian would never harm anyone. I—"

"No," the raw force of Lucan's denial halted her.

He continued his voice icy. "I will not hear of Calydon's innocence from you, when I know his guilt. It is time for you to leave, Constance."

Lucan rose to his feet with fluid grace and held out his hand helping her to stand. He rang the bell and instantly the door opened and the butler entered.

"You will be escorted to the side entrance so you are not seen. Be careful not to speak with anyone," he murmured, expression shuttered.

"Until I see you again, Lucan." She walked away, refusing to look back. He could not deny his passion for her, and she would wait for him to come to her. Certainly not forever, but she would give him enough time to realize the feelings he had for her would not simply vanish.

"Constance." Her name was just a whisper of sound but she heard it. She spun toward the door, and probed for Lucan in the soft shadows of the library.

"Marissa Alicia Wynwood."

Marissa. Constance hesitated, unsure if she should thank him for trusting her with this much. She knew it was his sister's name. But Constance did not know if she should feel glad that he shared a little more of himself, or fear that him revealing her name was part of some plan. Without speaking, she swept from the hall with hurried steps, very aware of the tender ache between her legs. Charlotte waited at the end of the hall looking a bit flushed and rumpled with Marcus Stone by her side, and Constance smiled in reassurance at Charlotte's worried frown. The hope in Constance's heart was heavy for she knew Lucan yearned for her with a similar intensity.

Now she only needed him to realize the love burgeoning between them was more worthy than vengeance.

Chapter Thirteen

The scandal that swept through town was the most exciting and satisfying society had ever heard, or at least it seemed that way to Constance. The Beautiful Bastard had been seen kissing the Lord of Sin, and at the club *Decadence* itself. It had been two days since the rumor, or better, the truth exploded. But a very strange truth for she knew no one could have possibly seen them enclosed in Lucan's office. Everyone in society was curious, for the Duke of Mondvale had not responded to the rumors, and there was certainly no news of an engagement published.

She had been puzzled when Charlotte handed over the paper she had been reading, her face white. Constance had scanned it quickly and right underneath the arts section in *The Spectator*, was a tattle on *her*. She had almost fainted. She could easily imagine the glee the hypocrites of the *haute monde* had expressed, sitting over their breakfast and reading of her latest sinful escapade. Constance could hardly credit it that someone had seen them. She had been in a mask and a wig and *all* kisses had been in private.

She had ridden out with her mother the morning after Charlotte had shared the scandal sheet. Constance had then understood the depth of her foolishness and what complete ruination meant. Several ladies that normally waved to her mother had given them both the cut direct. She had then been forced to reveal to her mother what had been published for all of London to see. Lady Radcliffe had swayed. Her mother had demanded to read the damming article herself.

> *Mrs. X has it on the highest authority that The Beautiful Bastard, Lady Constance, was seen kissing the Lord of Sin, Duke of Mondvale, at his club, Decadence. Most alarming to be sure, but not so unexpected. Mrs. X confirms that the Duke Mondvale has been seen with Lady Constance at Covent Garden and Hyde Park and wondered if a courtship had been going on.*

Her mother had gone white.

"Is this true, Connie?" had been the only question her mother had asked, and Constance's silence had been telling.

Her mother had walked away and the disappointment in her posture had pierced Constance. She had waited in dread and hope for Lucan to make an appearance at their town house, but his absence was very revealing. He really had no intention of calling on her despite the fact they had been seen.

Had he really decided his vengeance was more important? Tears burned behind her lids. How she wished he'd confided in her. She had spent the past couple of nights restless, wondering what had happened between his sister and Sebastian. How had she been driven to her death? Whatever occurred had been tragic enough where Lucan had planned to compromise Constance deliberately to hurt her brother. Though now it seems Lucan may be granted his wish, whether he had changed his mind or not. For if before she had been accorded any civility by the *haute monde* it would all be gone now. She was soiled, a wanton harlot the mammas would be protecting their daughters and sons from.

She laid her violin down on its stand as she heard the commotion from the hallway. She took a few calming breaths shoring up her courage. Her family had arrived. Sebastian and Jocelyn, Anthony and Phillipa. Her mother had summoned them to town and Constance had waited with a sick sense of fright for them to arrive.

She heard her parents' soft greeting and strained to hear her brothers' reply. Constance heard nothing. The door was swung open and Jocelyn barreled in, dressed in a dark yellow carriage dress, with her dark hair coiffed in an elegant chignon. She moved with energy despite her pregnant state and rushed over to Constance.

"Oh, Connie, I traveled up as soon as I heard. That wretched man," Jocelyn burst out, hugging her. Constance returned her embrace, her eyes prickling with tears. She looked over Jocelyn's head at the closed expression of both her brothers' faces. Phillipa was attired very casually in a purple walking dress with a hat perched jauntily on her head. She gave Constance an encouraging smile and walked over to her.

"Forgive me for being a watering pot." Jocelyn released her with a sniff. "I fear I have become somewhat emotional since the baby."

Constance hugged Phillipa briefly and everyone sat gathered in the parlor while her mother rang for tea. Mild pleasantries were exchanged but the air itself was fraught with tension. Constance did not fail to notice that her brothers had yet to say anything. She could feel their anger, even though they did nothing overt to show it. Their wives led the entire conversation and it was all about the mundane, though both Phillipa and Jocelyn wore the look of happily married women—certainly a rarity among the *haute monde.*

Mrs. Pritchard announced luncheon a few minutes later. With great reluctance, Constance entered the dining room. Her mother dismissed the footmen after they had been served. Constance waited with her stomach in knots. She knew they only gathered for one thing—to discuss the implications of her actions.

Her father wasted no time. "You know why we are all here, Connie. It is unpleasant business, but it must be dealt with. Your mother and I spoke at length and the decision we have made is that you must marry right away. Lord Litchfield will be calling on you tomorrow. I trust you will know what to do with his offer."

Constance took a few sips of her wine, her mind churning for a solution. It was as she feared. She shot Sebastian and Anthony a pleading look. She knew Sebastian would not fight with her father over his decision, but he was her guardian by law, not her mother's husband.

"The man who compromised her will be doing the marrying, Radcliffe," Sebastian interposed softly, but she could hear the implacable steel in his voice.

"I am marrying no one." The words slipped from Constance's lips before she even knew she would speak. "I was not compromised."

Cobalt blue eyes met hers, and she forced herself not to shrink away from Sebastian's ruthless will. She saw Jocelyn fleetingly touched his arm. He relaxed slightly as he laced his hands with hers beneath the table.

"Tell us what happened, pumpkin." Anthony invited with a smile, though his eyes remained cool and cautious. "I got mother's letter, but it was filled with ranting of how ruined we are. Why don't we hear from you what transpired? I know what the paper said, but we all know how notoriously unreliable they can be."

Constance opened her mouth, and the words still would not come.

"What happened, Constance?" Sebastian demanded at her continued silence.

She looked everywhere but at him. She couldn't bear to see his disappointment. Seconds flew by; then she shored up her courage and met his eyes. She flinched from his cold distant look. It was one he had never turned on her before. Her throat tightened as tears burned. "I visited *Decadence* for a private audience with the Duke of Mondvale."

Sebastian exhaled a slow breath, and she gathered how worried he must be. He nodded in encouragement. "Why?"

She fought to keep her face blank and buried the memories. It would not do for her to blush at all. "He called on me a few times, but at Lady Beaumont's ball he decided to terminate our friendship without any explanation. I thought it fair to demand answers."

Her mother's shocked inhalation had painful heat scorching Constance's skin.

"Were you seen kissing?" Sebastian demanded softly.

"No."

"Does it matter if she was seen?" her mother asked weakly. "The very fact that she visited that man in his club is enough. She is compromised. This is a terrible scandal. I doubt Connie will ever be able to recover from it."

Sebastian's anger seemed to pour over her in waves. "Did he touch you, Connie?"

She sucked in a harsh breath.

"We understand you are embarrassed," her father interjected, "but we must understand all that happened if we are to face it as a family."

She forced herself to look at everyone fully. It was not condemnation she saw but anger on her behalf and pity. It was the pity that gutted her and caused her hands to tremble. She clenched them tightly in her lap under the table. "He kissed me a few times."

"And?" the icy anger had not receded from Sebastian's voice.

She looked to Anthony for support and encountered a similarly cool gaze.

Anthony spoke at her hesitation. "It has been two days since this scandal, Connie, and Mondvale has not presented himself to ask for your hand. His reputation is…" He grimaced. "We need to know all that he did. Are you still a virgin, Connie?"

Her mother's fork clattered onto the table. "Anthony! This is not something we discuss so openly." Her face was florid.

"We need to understand what we are combating, Mother. Connie should have thought more of her sensibilities before she acted so impetuously," Sebastian snarled.

By a great effort of will, one Constance had never imagined she possessed, she tried to show an unreadable expression. "Yes,

I…I …believe so," she said before they could discuss the matter of her chastity anymore.

"You *believe* so?" Anthony asked with such lethal softness he unsettled her. "I must assume he went farther than kisses?"

Her face burned, and she wanted to sink underneath the table. She was not sure if there was more to the act than what they had done. Lucan had touched and kissed her in a place she didn't even know she could be touched. But there must be more, because Lucan had still seemed so tensed and unfulfilled. Not that she would ever admit to such a thing! Resolutely she thrust Lucan and her improper behavior from mind. She looked to Phillipa for help. The anger burning in her gaze as she looked at Anthony comforted Constance.

"I would think if Connie is in doubt my lords, *nothing* happened," Jocelyn growled. "You will both cease embarrassing her further."

Constance could feel the relief that traveled through her brothers and even her father, and her shame burned brighter. For if not for Lucan's restraint, as he told her before, he would have gone further. She had failed them all with her behavior.

"Then why are you crying?" Anthony demanded.

She raised a hand to her cheek, and swiped away the wetness she found. "My nerves must be more unsettled than I realized."

He nodded, accepting her inane explanation, but his face had softened.

"What are we to do, Sebastian? Lady Blade saw us both today, and as I walked over to greet her, she turned away." The mortification in her mother's voice was rife.

The memory had Constance's head pounding, and she reached for her glass of water. *I was so foolish.*

"You can plan for a June wedding, madam," Sebastian said calmly. Too calmly.

Horror burned in Constance's veins.

"Why do you look so surprised, Connie? You think I would allow someone to compromise you and not marry you?"

She straightened in her chair. "I do not wish to marry Mondvale under such circumstances, Sebastian, and I am certain he will not marry me. I cannot imagine what happened, for I am certain I was not seen, I swear to you, and he did not compromise me."

"The fact that he kissed you, *touched* you was enough," Sebastian's voice was implacable.

She shifted her glance to Anthony and espied the same resolve. Sudden fear filled her. She knew with a deep bone certainty that Lucan would never bend to their will. She could not imagine her brothers giving up either. Constance did not want to marry Lucan like this. "I do not want to marry him," she said hoarsely. *Liar*, her heart taunted. She yearned for Lucan, but if he came to her this way they would never have a happy marriage. She was sure of it, but she was not sure if she had any choice either.

"If you do not wish to wed Mondvale I will not force you. But you will accept Litchfield's offer. Either way you will be married by June."

She searched Sebastian's face. There was no hint of humor.

"The option is to marry, or live your life as a recluse in disgrace in the country," her mother said quietly.

"We must rally as if nothing happened," Phillipa interjected, her golden eyes flashing with anger. "From what I have seen of society, if you flee to the country it is an admission of guilt. I am sure that is not the right way." Phillipa said glancing at Anthony.

"But why has Mondvale not presented himself here? He must have known the risk when he allowed Constance entrance into his club?" Jocelyn demanded.

"Mayhap he thought Connie was trying to compromise him?" Phillipa ventured. "More than one mamma has tried it this past season and has been met with a similar response."

Her mother sniffed delicately. "He is a reprobate, that is why. Uncaring and cruel. I knew he was not good enough for Connie, but I foolishly allowed him to call on her without declaring his intentions."

Lucan was not uncaring and cruel, more stubborn and foolish. Constance had seen the naked need on his face for her. She had also seen how he tried to push her away. She took some comfort in thinking it meant he had hated hurting her. Though it was hollow comfort, indeed.

He was trying to close his heart to her because he believed implicitly in her brother's guilt. To shatter Lucan's reserve she needed to understand what had happened. If he would not confide her in, mayhap Sebastian would. "Marissa Alicia Wynwood," she said.

The blood drained from Jocelyn's face and the arctic blast from Sebastian's closed face chilled Constance. *What is it?* The depth of fear that filled her, made her head swam. The torment and rage behind Lucan's eyes as he had uttered the words now seemed more real and not a figment of her imagination.

"Who is she?" Constance questioned into the fraught silence.

"Where did you hear her name?" Sebastian questioned.

A part of her wanted to hold it back. For she suddenly knew this was Lucan's intention. He knew the name would galvanize Sebastian.

"Constance?"

"How do you know her, Sebastian?" She could see that they all knew. Even her father.

"Until you inform me how it is you came to mention her name, I will not divulge who Marissa was."

How could Lucan believe Sebastian had something to do with her death?

"That was the last thing Luc—His Grace said to me. I demanded as to why he would terminate our friendship and his answer was her name. She was his sister, I believe—"

"Oh my Goodness!" Jocelyn breathed, as everyone fell silent.

"His full name and title is Lucan Devlin Wynwood, the Duke of Mondvale," Anthony said carefully as he looked at Sebastian.

Constance could feel the undercurrent of emotions arching from her brother and wrapping him into a bubble she did not understand. She also saw the pain in his eyes, it was real and deep. Who had Marissa been to him?

Jocelyn looked a little pale, but she gave him a sweet supporting smile.

"Who was she to you, Sebastian?" Constance asked, her heart squeezing.

"A friend."

She waited, but he revealed nothing else. "Please do not shut me out."

She could see him closing off and knew she would get nothing from him further.

"I am not feeling so well," Jocelyn murmured, laying down her serviette. Her words had the desired effect of rousing Sebastian. He pushed back from his chair and gently eased her up.

Constance met his gaze, wanting to demand an explanation.

"We will speak later, Constance," he promised.

She nodded, grateful he no longer seemed so angry with her. But she was not sure she liked what she saw in his eyes either.

Guilt.

Chapter Fourteen

Constance laid on the chaise, snuggled under a blanket, her mind in deep turbulence. The fire in the grate had died to mere embers, but she lacked the energy to ring for a servant. She hated disturbing anyone this late anyway. She should have been in her bed. Instead, she had waited until the household fell asleep before retiring to the library to read. The tension and the uncertainty had left her feeling miserable, and she had sought to lose herself in a novel.

Sebastian had made no effort to speak with her, and even her father had rebuffed her plea for understanding. Worse, Lucan still had not called on her.

She had no memory of falling asleep, and her foggy mind tried to make out what woke her. She looked to the fallen book on the floor, wondering if it was the thud of it dropping from her hand that had roused her. Then she heard a sound and glanced sideways to see Sebastian and Anthony entering the library. What were they doing? She opened her mouth to speak when Anthony's words froze her.

"The Duke of Mondvale is Marissa's brother," incredulity rang in Anthony's voice.

Sebastian expelled a deep breath and sank onto the sofa nearest to the fire, stretching his long legs out in a casual and relaxed pose. He had but to turn his head and probe the shadows in the far corner of the library to make out her curled form on the chaise. "I thought Marissa a ghost I had successfully exorcized from my mind and heart," Sebastian admitted.

Constance's breath caught, the intention to reveal her presence stifled.

"Constance is in love with him."

"Why do you say that?" Sebastian all but snarled.

Anthony's soft chuckle held no humor. "Connie would never have allowed Mondvale any liberties if she did not fancy herself in love with him, Sebastian. Did you see her face each time she spoke of him? She tried to appear indifferent, but she failed. He mattered enough for her to risk visiting his club to demand answers. That is revealing and very much like Connie. I do not think it wise to insist she marry Lord Litchfield."

They went silent as if contemplating.

"It savages me to see her in pain," Sebastian finally replied. "But she must marry."

She thought she had been so successful in hiding her true feelings.

A sigh heaved from Anthony, and his shadow pushed off from the bookcase and went to sit on the far end of the sofa beside Sebastian, but much closer to her.

"Connie is not a reckless fool, Sebastian. For some

reason, she decided she wanted the Duke of Mondvale. Not Litchfield who has offered for her three time now. Though we know the size of her inheritance has something to do with his persistence. Connie tends to know what she wants in life and pursues it single-mindedly. Do you remember when she was young how determined she had been for the old duke to love her? It had been a painful thing to watch but she had not given up in the face of his coldness. She pushed even when I faltered. She showed that same tenacity when she learned to ride, fence, play the violin, and speak languages. We should have expected it to be the same in the pursuit of her prince charming—as she called her future husband from the age of twelve."

Tears slipped down Constance's face as she listened to her brothers. It was even more imperative they know she was listening before they said something that had the power to shatter her. She never realized how much they saw into her, cared for her. She could hear the depth of love in Anthony's voice as he spoke. Words begged to tumble from her lips, but she remained frozen.

"Do you really believe she is untouched?" Sebastian growled. "We know full well how passion can burn out of control. And it is damned difficult to think of Connie as a woman with desires."

Embarrassment burned inside of her, and she waited for Anthony's reply in an agony of humiliation.

"Any woman would know if she had made love, Sebastian, but from her mortification I *can* say he did more than chaste kissing."

She could not make out Sebastian's response but she certainly heard his soft snarl.

They were silent for the longest time, then Sebastian

spoke. "Mondvale must believe I had something to do with Marissa's death. I cannot bear the idea of seeing Connie's pain, nor can I accept forcing her to wed where her heart does not lie. It will only hurt her further. But I cannot ignore her being in his club, without a doubt compromised, and not wed. I failed her. I should have traveled up with her from Sherring Cross. I knew she did not wish to return to town, and I allowed her to face society's censure alone."

It felt as if a fist closed over her heart at Sebastian's assertion.

"Do not be foolish," Anthony snapped. "No one expected you to leave Jocelyn when she was feeling so ill. I was the one who should have been here. But we had been suffocating her, and it was a hard thing to give her space. In fact, I prefer to lay the blame at the feet of the man who allowed her entrance into his club. If he cared anything for her, he would have made an offer the minute her presence in his club became known to society."

And therein lies the heart of the problem, the torment that had made Constance so uneasy. Lucan cared not how damaged her reputation had truly gotten. Nothing would force him to wed the sister of his enemy.

Sebastian sighed. "I think that is because of Marissa. What did you learn from your investigation?"

Constance's heart lurched. Sebastian had Anthony investigate Lucan? When? The scandal only broke two days ago. Her brothers must have been in motion the instant they received their mother's letter saying she had been ruined by the Duke of Mondvale. She knew as the Duke of Calydon, Sebastian was powerful, and he had the resources to find out all he wanted on Lucan. Even things Lucan would want buried.

"He started in London's underbelly and rose to be

a shipping magnate in ten years. He also has significant investments in steamships and lands. He is wealthy and powerful, and that was before he inherited the dukedom," Anthony said. "He inherited the title last year. Before then he spent most of his time in the Orient and the Americas. His mother, Lady Natalee, is the previous Duke of Mondvale's daughter who had ran off with her tutor. She was disinherited. And the duke died without any more issues. It took the crown almost four years to find Mondvale."

Constance was amazed at what her brothers had been able to unearth so quickly.

"He owns the gaming club *Decadence*?" Sebastian queried.

Paper shuffled and her eyes strained. She prayed they would not turn on the gas light in the room. It would be very hard for her to brazen her way out. Though she could pretend she was asleep. As if that would fool her two astute brothers.

"He is one fourth owner along with the Earl of Ainsley, a man they simply call the Reverend, but who is indeed the Viscount of Trent's disinherited son, and one Sir Marcus Stone," Anthony said.

"It is said here that he is very influential, in what manner?"

She swallowed, waiting for Anthony's reply. Her legs cramped from being folded. She gently shifted and bit her lip to prevent her cry as blood rushed through her limbs.

Anthony spoke, "Calvert said Mondvale's reputation is not to be taken lightly."

"How is it possible that one man amassed this much power and remained virtually unheard of?"

She heard the click of glasses and saw shadows moving by the mantel. How they were able to pour drink into glasses with only the light from the dying fireplace flummoxed her.

"Mayhap that was by his design. His wealth does not compare to the Calydon holdings. But he trades in secrets and information thus he is valuable to many," Anthony murmured.

"Enemies?" Sebastian asked.

"The man is careful," Anthony growled. "What are you thinking?"

"He will marry Constance or I will destroy him," Sebastian vowed. "I will speak with him about Marissa. I did not even know she had a brother, Anthony. I wonder if she was ever truthful about anything."

Constance's heart froze at the menace in Sebastian's tone. *No*. Her mind and heart screamed in denial.

"What manner of man is he for our sister?"

"His reputation as a ruthless businessman is vaunted. His relentless rise to power and influence had been admired by society, and his inheritance of the title had unwittingly been the final touch to his masterpiece. When it had become known that the 'Lord of Sin' was the Duke of Mondvale, he was sought after for more than money and vice. Ambitious *maters* wanted him for their daughters and some even tried to compromise him. He did not bow to convention and marry any of them. Connie needs someone gentle, someone—" Anthony's voice held a note of frustration. "He may be a duke, Sebastian, but I cannot see someone like Mondvale with Connie. From all accounts he is jaded and hard-hearted. It is said he is ruthless to those that antagonize him, which you have clearly done with this business with Marissa. I would hate for all those feelings of his to be directed at our sister. I do not think it wise to force her to marry him, even if she loves him."

"If I do not, she will be ruined."

Constance stuffed a fist in her mouth to prevent her sob. More than anything she wished she had not stayed. *Ruined.* Her brothers thought her disgraced. They would definitely not rest until she was wed, and Lucan would not bow to their will. She knew it with every fiber of her being. That meant she would be persuaded to wed Litchfield. Bile rose in her throat and despair shafted through her heart. She would not do it. She had never rebelled against her brothers' gentle directions before, but she would not enter a union so permanent, so sacred, with a man she did not love or even possess a morsel of affection for.

"Connie is already perceived as ruined," Anthony countered bluntly. "The circumstances of our birth do not lie in our favor. And now this. Phillipa and I were planning to travel to Italy and then Egypt in a few weeks. Why not have Connie accompany us? Give her some respite from England, away from it all. She is young, and there will be time aplenty for her to find her prince charming."

Hope and gratefulness suffused her at Anthony's words. She held her breath waiting for Sebastian's reply.

"I will discuss traveling with you and Phillipa with Connie," Sebastian murmured.

"Good. Are you going to explain to her about Marissa?"

"It doesn't concern her."

Anthony snorted.

"I cannot explain to our sister that Marissa was my mistress who killed herself when I refused to be with her," Sebastian snapped.

Lucan's word filtered in her mind with brutal clarity. *Calydon used my sister and then abandoned her.* No it couldn't be true. There must be something more.

"It was a little more than that," Anthony said drily. "Marissa asked you to help her be free of her husband. I think any sane man would have said no to murder."

Good heavens.

Constance hardly knew what to do with all she was hearing. Her brothers were silent and a soft breath eased from her when Anthony asked about Jocelyn and the babe. Mistress? Murder? It was all too much. A part of her now understand why Sebastian had refused to speak with her and had studiously avoided her the entire day. Everything he did was about protecting her. When would he realize she was no longer a child? She needed to know this. And she instinctively knew, if not for tonight, she would never have been made aware of the details.

What was he really concerned with? Protecting her innocence — or protecting the love and belief she had in him?

Chapter Fifteen

Lucan had not thought there was anything his friends could do to render him speechless, and he was not a man easily surprised.

"You did what?" he asked for the second time, certain he had been mistaken.

Even the Reverend looked flummoxed, and he was the most unflappable one of their depraved group. The Reverend's obsidian eyes were carefully void of all emotions as he looked at both Lucan and Ainsley.

"I leaked a story of Lady Constance being seen here to my inside source at *The Spectator*. It was run two mornings ago. You were away on business in Derbyshire, and I realized you were not aware of the situation. Here is the sheet in the event you wish to read it," Ainsley murmured at bit warily.

With a calmness Lucan did not feel, he picked up the paper and read the notice. He went cold. *She is ruined.* He already knew how the scandal would be received by society.

Because of his wealth and title he would be forgiven. Instead of calling him out for his reprehensible actions of having her in his club and kissing her, the mammas of the *haute monde* would applaud his good sense in escaping the trap the bastard girl had set for him.

He fought down the rage that bit at his insides and buried his emotions deep. He did not know what Ainsley saw when he looked at him, but the man was smart enough to step back a few paces and held up his hand.

"Hear me out, Lucan."

"I do not think there is anything to hear. You have taken steps to ruin her further, after I changed my path. She will not be able to recover from this. Why would you act so maliciously toward her?"

"Lucan, I—"

"Hold your fucking tongue," Lucan snarled. "I trusted you and you betrayed my confidence."

"I thought it was the only way—"

Within two strides he stood in front of Ainsley, grabbed him by his collar, and slammed him into the bookcase. The violence tearing through Lucan's gut begged for an outlet, and he ruthlessly struggled against smashing Ainsley's teeth into his thick skull. "The only way for what?"

Ainsley gripped the hands fisting his collar. "For you to let go of this vengeance and marry the woman you hold such obvious affections for. I can see how you feel about her. I have never seen anyone leave you in such knots. And you are not just one of us anymore. You are now a duke, Lucan, *a duke*. I have seen you happy for the first time in years. I could think of no other way to get you to direct your happiness toward her. And I know you are pig-headed enough to let her slip through your fingers. But I also know how much you care for her, and those affections you have for her would never allow you to truly see her ruined."

Lucan pushed Ainsley away, damn the man for trying to manipulate him. For once again, it was Constance paying the price. "How do you think she is not completely ruined now?"

"If you marry her, society will forgive her. You are the Duke of Mondvale, you know. But better, you are the Lord of Sin. You provide the means for high society to satiate their appetite for the sinful and forbidden. They secretly love you for it. As your duchess, she will be unable to fall to ruin."

Lucan knew the truth of it. If her brothers had been able to wed her to a duke, possibly all he had been doing from the shadows would have been prevented. For as he understood, the realm had less than thirty dukes and most were married and doddering. As a duchess, she would command respect despite being the Beautiful Bastard. But could he do it? Combine his family with the man who had callously contributed to the ruin of a most beloved sister?

Everything in him rebelled against the idea. To wed her, he would have to forgive Calydon. "I will not forgive you anytime soon for this, Ainsley," Lucan promised. The hurt and condemnation she must be facing now was insupportable.

"I know you will demand satisfaction for this, Lucan. I will meet you in the ring for several bouts tonight," Ainsley offered. "But this was the only way I could think of to get you to stop behaving so foolishly and claim the woman your heart has chosen."

Without speaking, Lucan grabbed his coat and top hat and swept from the room. He would fix this, but certainly not in the manner Ainsley expected.

• • •

"The *Duke of Mondvale* is here?" Constance asked Mr. Harris for the third time.

"Yes, my lady."

Good heavens.

Why had he come? She was the only one at home. Should she see him? Not even Charlotte was present, having left earlier in a secretive rush. "Have you informed His Grace that Lord and Lady Radcliffe are not at home?"

Mr. Harris gave her a slight smile and nod. "I was once again informed he wishes to speak with Lady Constance."

She nodded. "I will see him in the gardens outside. If my parents return before he leaves, please inform them of our whereabouts." She would not see him at all in private, and she had intended to take a turn in the gardens to collect some flowers for the drawing room.

"I understand, my lady."

With a calm she had not expected, she went upstairs and collected her shawl. Within a few minutes, she was in the gardens walking toward the stone bench on which he sat. Gravel crunched beneath her feet and Lucan stood to face her. She had missed him. Today he was dressed in a gray suit, his hair once again caught in a queue. He adjusted his spectacles on his nose — a nervous gesture she was learning to identify.

"Your Grace," she intoned formally with a slight curtsy. "To what do I owe your unexpected visit?"

His eyes roamed over her almost hungrily, before resting

on her face. "Are you well?" he asked quietly.

"I am, thank you."

"I was made aware of the publication in the papers only this morning. I had been away on business and returned to town today."

Relief surged through her. He was not so uncaring after all.

A smile lifted her lips. "I see. And you hastened to visit me because?" she prompted, her heart beating a bit faster.

He hesitated. "If you want to marry it will be done."

She stiffened. "Are you proposing?"

He winced. "No. But it was pointed out to me that marriage is the only option for you. I agree."

She stared at him in outrage. "So you agree I need to marry, but not to you?"

"Yes."

She wondered if she spoke with the same man who had danced with her beneath the stars that had kissed her, that had made her feel so much. "And who do you suppose I should marry? I do not see a bevy of suitors calling on me."

"Make a list of anyone you desire. Whether it be an earl or a duke or a baron. He will marry you."

Constance glared at him. He really wanted her to marry someone else. He could relinquish her so easily? "That is not possible. I am ruined." *By my own foolish desire for you*, her heart screamed, but she refused to show him any emotions. She would die before she gave him an inkling of knowledge of how much his disinterest was hurting her.

"I will make it so."

"How?" she whispered harshly. "My brother is the Duke of Calydon, and I can assure you he cannot simply tell me to pick a name from society."

"Your brother doesn't own anyone."

She stared at him appalled. Own anyone? *Good heavens.* "Such a gesture on your part is unnecessary."

"If not for my attentions you would have not been in such a situation. You were not seen, but a misguided friend revealed the information that you were at *Decadence* hoping to force my hand. I will do all in my power to make reparations. If there is anything you want, and it is in my power, I will get it for you. You only have to say the words. And I pray that you will see this as a token of how deeply regretful I am."

She nodded mutely, her heart a painful cadence inside of her chest. "Thank you. Do you really care about my happiness, Lucan?"

"Nothing is more important to me. Whatever you want, whatever you need, if it is within my power you will have it, Constance."

Hope curled inside of her, yet she hesitated.

"What do you want, Constance?"

She braced herself. "You."

Constance never imagined he would be so surprised at her declaration. Everything about him seemed frozen. Before she lost her nerves she expounded. "I will be your duchess."

He went so unemotionally distant he shook her calm facade. But she would not plead with him.

"No," he growled.

She nodded. "Then I bid you good-bye, Your Grace."

She walked away from him with quiet calm. She would not wed someone she did not love. If he would not have her, she would travel with Anthony and Phillipa and see some of the world. She would not commit to a life of unhappiness to please society or even her mother, who had traveled a similar path that had led them to near ruination. Constance would not repeat her mother's mistake.

Her heart lurched as hands gently encircled her waist from behind. She had not heard him move at all. She tensed. "Why are you touching me?"

He released her as if he had been stung, and she slowly turned to face him, curious to what she would see. *Oh, Lucan.* Emotions roiled in his eyes, and she saw the flash of fear before he buried it. She waited for him to speak, without any expectations in her heart.

. . .

Lucan felt a horrible sense of inevitability pressed in on him. "I will not marry you," he reiterated softly.

"You have already said so," Constance pointed out, her demeanor one of calm and indifference.

She stepped back from him, her pale pink skirt swirling in a gentle manner around her feet. An unidentifiable emotion swept through him. She did not comprehend how much he had influenced the pain she and her family now suffered. She also knew nothing about him. He had built his fortune on the sins of others'. Not only did they owe him a great deal of money, but Lucan had made it his business to know about others weaknesses. He never did anything with the knowledge, only alerting the unsuspecting fool when he needed him for something. As he had done with Lord Orwell. If she knew the depth of Lucan's crimes against her, she would not be so open to marrying him. He opened his mouth to inform her, but everything inside of him shut down for seconds. He could not bear for the look in her eyes to turn to contempt and hatred.

His heart lurched at the thought of her discovering his secrets. He had known loathing and bitterness, but fear no longer had the power to touch him, or so he had thought. For he felt fear now that she would see all of him and be repulsed. "You do not know the manner of man I am, Constance. To want to wed me is a naive, foolish desire after how I planned to compromise you. I am incapable of giving you the kind of marriage—the kind of love—you seem to desire."

Her chin titled, and damn if she wasn't staring him down despite her head barely reaching his chest.

"And what kind of marriage do I need, Your Grace?"

He hesitated then spoke frankly. "One with love and laughter, picnics and balls, children and merriment…and family solidarity."

"And why is it you cannot give me that?"

"Because all I have left inside since I lost Marissa is darkness."

She shifted closer to him. "That has an easy solution. I cannot bring back your sister, and the ache of her loss will be with you for years to come, but I will take some of your darkness and give you my light. I will always comfort you when you feel pain."

He looked at her in bemusement. Take his darkness? The last thing he wanted was for her to understand the depth of his demons. "I want you nowhere near my wickedness."

Constance flushed. "I know you are not as dissolute as you would have me believe, Lucan."

"Is that so?"

She gave him a rather wistful smile, and he wanted to give her the things she dreamed of. "I know about the Edinburgh Review articles that you write, championing humanitarian views of ending the practice of farming babies. I am aware of the motions you take to parliament. I know about your many charities. I know you did not ruin me when everything in you clamored to; instead you tried to protect me. So you see, I *know* of the good in you."

The silence was deafening.

"You may well be wondering how I know this, but I do read," she said in a teasing manner. "My brothers firmly believed in my education, and while I tend to indulge in penny dreadfuls and romantic novels, I also edify my mind with sensible reading. I have read all the arguments you have put forth. I admire them, and I believe they tell me a lot of your character, Lucan. And I see much to be admired."

Much to be admired? Unable to face her hopefulness anymore, he turned away and closed his eyes.

He did not deserve her. Fear gripped his heart in the most unwelcomed manner. He wanted to reach out so badly and claim what she offered. A life with her. But he could never allow himself to become enmeshed with her, for the moment she found out the depth of his actions against her family, against her, she would despise him. And then he would know true pain.

For he was already in love with her.

Then why are you thinking of walking away you fool, his conscience screamed. *You love her.*

"Lucan?" her voice was soft as she touched his back with a feather light caress.

He groaned stifling the impulse to draw her into his arms and crush her lips to his. Though he fought hard against it, he'd had a startling realization during the early morning train ride to London — he needed Constance in his life. He'd missed her fiercely in the few days apart.

He felt as if it would take months, perhaps even years before the ache of Calydon's involvement in his sister's death diminished. But he had to consider, more so than ever before, that the man should not be held as deeply in contempt as Marissa's husband who abused her so cruelly. The night Constance had visited *Decadence*, Lucan had reread all fifty-six of Marissa's letters. And then he had burned them one by one. All her hopes and fears, her pain and desperation had been infused in those words, and he refused to remember her that way anymore. He'd acknowledged what he had fought against for so long. Marissa had been as flawed as everyone else. She had taken a lover after marriage. A thing he had not thought his sweet sister capable of. He did not judge her for it, he only saw how much he had failed her.

And he only knew because she wrote how Calydon spurned her after taking her innocence, and that in her anger she wedded Stanhope. Then she had continued her affair with Calydon. She had told Lucan how her husband had beaten and tormented her after he realized she was still seeing Calydon. Lucan had been in the Americas when he received that letter, he had almost expired from horror, and traveled back to London immediately. But while he had been traveling back he intercepted her last letter to him, and realized he had lost his sister.

To now relinquish his anger against Calydon, and to recognize that he must have been as young and reckless as Marissa, was an idea that would take Lucan years to resolve. But he was willing to try, for Constance's sake. He had to try.

"Lucan?"

He faced her and cupped her cheeks. Her eyes flared

wide and the hope in them made his chest constricted. He was a damnable fool to make such a treasure slip from his grasp because of fear. "I was an insufferable ass for suggesting you wed another, forgive me." He moved closer to her. "Will you marry me, Constance?"

A grin split her face. "Yes."

There was no hesitation, and the surety of her response and the joy in her eyes humbled him. He would endeavor to make her the happiest of woman.

"I will visit tomorrow and call upon your father, then I will speak with your brother."

She nodded, then laughed, infecting him with her happiness. Lucan dipped his head and pressed a soft kiss against her lips, burying the need to blurt the truth of his involvement in her pain and ostracism from society. He would unburden all to her, but not today. A deep part of him wished he would never have to reveal it, but he would not start their life together with deception.

For now, he basked in the sweetness of her kiss and the comfort of her touch, knowing he would face the day he had to reveal *all* his sins to her.

Chapter Sixteen

The cheery gathering in the breakfast room was for Constance's benefit. She understood that, and loved her family for their support, but she pled a headache and took a tray into her room. She wanted to tell her family Lucan would be calling, but knew it was best to remain silent. While he had promised to speak with her father, he had not mentioned anything in relation to his sister and Sebastian. It was as if Lucan simply closed away the raw grief she had seen in his eyes, where she knew it would simmer and seethe with the possibility of exploding into something horrible one day. They all needed to discuss it as a family, but no one was confiding in her. She hoped after Lucan called on her father and brother, an amicable resolution would be found.

With the need beating in her to understand the rife between her love and her brother, she had sought out Jocelyn, and spoke of what had been overheard between Sebastian and Anthony in the library. Constance had also told her of Lucan's visit, and all that had been said between them after securing her promise to remain silent. Jocelyn had in turn tried to shed some light on Marissa and Sebastian's relationship. Constance did not comprehend fully what paramours did, but what made it all more shocking was that Marissa had been married. Sebastian had an affair with a married woman. Constance could hardly credit it.

It had not been easy for Jocelyn to speak, Constance had seen that. And she had been grateful Jocelyn had confided in her. For Constance had already realized Sebastian would omit the details. Before breakfast she and Sebastian had taken a turn in the gardens where he had shared some of his past with her. He told her Marissa had been his dear friend whom he lost. *Dear friend.* Constance had bitten her lips so as not to blurt out that she was well aware of what Lucan's sister was to him, and that there was no need to spare her the details.

She looked at the folder gripped so tightly in her hands. *Do I want to know?*

She had not meant to eavesdrop on her brothers *again.* She had only intended to confess to Sebastian that she had overheard him and Anthony, and to ask him to somehow resolve the storm that was still brewing between him and Lucan. It had also been her intention to inform him that Lucan would be offering for her. She'd heard Anthony informing Sebastian that the report on Lucan was completed. She'd had no intention of stealing the report until Anthony asked if they should inform her of what they found. Sebastian's "no" had been unequivocal. Disappointment and frustration had surged in her. Even with everything crumbling around them, her brothers still thought it necessary to withhold information.

She had made quick work of stealing into Sebastian's chamber and finding the folder. She knew she needed to read it and discreetly return it before breakfast was over. Constance sat on the chaise in her chamber, ignoring the food on the small table by the window. She flipped open the report, amazed at what had been gleaned in as little as three days.

Fifteen minutes later, she slowly closed the file, her heart beating so hard she feared she would faint. She had never meant anything to Lucan. The torment that had followed her since last year had been orchestrated by him.

The anger that gripped Constance was better than the cold pain snaking around her heart. What a fool she had been. With a distant sort of calmness she walked to Jocelyn and Sebastian's chamber, entered, and replaced the folder in the top drawer of the chest. She returned to her room, and sat in the high wingback chair looking out the window that faced the small but beautiful garden.

The tears would not come. She felt incapable of crying. The hurt was too much. She felt as if a dagger had been plunged inside of her and was still knifing through her with vicious intensity. She had been filled with much romantic idiocy of a prince charming wooing and sweeping her off her feet. A prince charming she had been so sure was Lucan. Constance vowed then, never would she allow her heart to be open to another man.

· · ·

Lucan alighted from his carriage, not liking the feelings of nervousness wafting through him. He was not the type of man to be affected by nerves. *Bloody hell*. He'd been unable to sleep after leaving Constance and had spent better part of the night boxing bare knuckle with Ainsley, and then Marcus. Yet tension still wound Lucan tight. While he had all intention of offering for Constance, he would not call on her father, until Lucan had unburdened all to her. It was damn tempting to bind her in marriage to him, then reveal his complicity in her pain. But the thought of once again deceiving her left a sour taste in his mouth. He would first speak with her and beg her forgiveness for his past actions, then he would speak to her father and Calydon.

Lucan had glimpsed her blond hair from his carriage, pacing in the gardens. He avoided the front of the townhouse and walked to the side gate where he quietly entered. Luckily the gate was unlatched. He walked on the stone path toward her. Dressed in a peach day dress, and with her unbound hair rippling to her waist, Lucan thought she had never looked more ravishing.

"Constance."

She jerked and spun around to face him, her hand pressing against her chest.

"Forgive me if I startled you."

"What are you doing here?" No excitement lighted her eyes or her voice. She sounded bland. She looked behind him to the gate and then back toward the house.

He frowned. "I am to call on your father, but I first wanted to speak with you on an urgent matter."

"And you did not think that you should call at the front?"

"I wanted to converse without any interruption from your family. I understand they are all here?"

She closed her eyes almost as if in pain and walked farther into the garden. When it seemed as if she determined they were far enough away to be accorded full privacy, she looked at him.

"My brothers and their wives are not here. However, my father is in his study and my mother in the parlor."

Her stare was filled with a curious state of detachment. Concern curled through him. "Are you well, Constance?"

"Why would I not be? Tell me, Your Grace, what is this urgent matter you wish to discuss? " she asked icily.

Your Grace? Whatever happened to referring to me as Lucan? He took a few steps closer to her. "Before I start I want you to know how much I love you and—"

"Love?"

She looked at him as if she had never seen him before. It was not the look of sweetness and want that he was used to seeing from her.

"Yes… I do, more so than I thought possible, but before I speak of the affections I hold for you, I need to confess my sins and hope that you will forgive me. Then if you will have me, I—"

"Your Grace, I—"

"Let me finish—"

"I cannot!"

Her hands fisted at her side and what flashed in her eyes was pure rage. His gut knotted in a way it had never before, and the cold chill that slithered through Lucan was alarming.

She took a deep breath and firmed her shoulders. Her head tilted and she met his gaze. "I cannot listen as you spout to me sentiments of love and affection, Your Grace. It would be cruel for me to allow you to express yourself and lay your heart bare when I have no intention of returning your regard *ever*."

Lucan felt the ground shift under his feet, and he crushed the hat in his hands. Had he been mistaken in her affections for him? He could not have been. She had expressly told him of her love, kissed him, and surrendered her passion to him so ardently. Did she believe he was crying off?

"I have all intention of asking Lord Radcliffe for your hand, Constance. I wish to marry you. If it is that you doubt I—"

"*Marriage*? What makes you think I could ever be persuaded to marry you?" she asked with such withering scorn it drew him up. "Your Grace, I beg of you to leave and forget the conversation we had yesterday. I will not tell my family you called. I am too ashamed of my naivety to tell the truth of my situation to anyone."

Her eyes glistened with tears, but her lips were firm with determination. He felt gutted. The lack of any tender regards in her gaze hurt him far worse than he could have ever imagined.

What makes you think I could ever be persuaded to marry you? "Tell me why you will not marry me. If this is because of my foolish words yesterday I—"

Her expression became even more unreadable. "Goodbye, Your Grace." She spun and made to exit the garden.

He grabbed her hand, halting her retreat.

She rounded on him like a tigress. "You will not touch me again without my consent, Your Grace, and I can assure you it will *never* be given."

Lucan released her. "Tell me what happened," he demanded. "When I was foolish enough to discourage you from me, you pursued me all the way to my club demanding an answer. Answers I gave truthfully. I now demand to know why you reject my offer, and let me inform you, Lady Constance, you do not want me pursuing you for the truth."

She vibrated with indignation. "I owe you no such courtesy, but I will tell you, and then you may never darken my doorstep again. Do you think I could marry the man that deliberately left me open to ridicule and scorn? The man who sought to use me so cruelly to exact revenge against my brother? All your kisses were lies. Our laughter and passion were lies. The thing that has hurt me most was revealed by *you*. And it was all done so spitefully. *You* told the world of my bastardy, Lucan."

A harsh sob ripped from her, and she pressed her fist into her stomach. Tears ran down her cheeks, and her voice went hoarse. "You have brought hurt to me and my family in the most abominable way. I have no friends. We are not called upon. My mother and I were given the cut direct too many times to count, and this repulsion from society was done by *your* design. Yet you stand here and tell me you love me and you wish to marry me? You have no heart to bear affections, Your Grace."

Everything inside of him crumbled. He stepped closer to her. "Constance, please let me explain. I had all intentions of telling you today how incredibly stupid I have been and to beg your forgiveness. I—"

She stumbled away from him, and he dropped the hand he had held out in entreaty.

She drew herself up, though he could see what it cost her to hold onto her composure. She seemed brittle, as if she was holding on from breaking down and screaming at him. "There is nothing for you to explain. I understand enough. You told me your sister was ruined and driven to her death. For that I cannot express enough sympathy despite the fact that I did not know her. She must have been lovely to command such depth of love and loyalty, where you would be driven to ruin another in a similarly cold and cruel fashion. You are heartless to hold me accountable for the sins of others, Your Grace. For while my brother was a young foolish man to have been embroiled with a married woman, your sister must have been fully aware she was also a married woman having an affair!"

Lucan fought to stave off the anger that washed over him. "Do not speak ill of my sister, or of a situation I can see you still do not comprehend," he snarled.

She jerked back, her eyes wide and her frame trembling.

He slapped his hat against his thigh, burying the flare of emotions. It would not do for the two of them to be in such a state. "Condemn me if you must, hate me if you must, but do not breathe a word that would taint Marissa's character further after all your brother has done. You judge me, and I deserve your reproach, but she does not. You claim your brother was a young and foolish man, only misguided, but I am cruel and heartless for attempting to do the same thing he himself executed on my sister?"

Constance sucked in a harsh breath. "You dare compare my brother's actions to those of yours? You have used me in the most hurtful of ways. What was his error but in loving a woman that was already married? I do not seek to besmirch your sister's good name, I only seek to defend my brother whom you hold in such contempt."

"Your brother took my sister's innocence then *refused* to marry her. Her connections were too low for him to make her his duchess. But not low enough to keep her as his mistress even after she wed. But his greatest crime against her, was that he abandoned her when she needed him. Has your beloved brother explained his actions to you? For I will never see them in a favorable and forgiving light."

She shook her head as if in a daze. "Yet you want to marry me with such continued contempt for my family? I think, Your Grace, it is yourself you are unable to forgive."

Lucan jerked as if she had slapped him.

Tears split down her cheeks. "Do not leave thinking you have not had your revenge on my brother. You succeeded well. If you wanted to hurt me as how he must have hurt your sister, you have succeeded. That you set out to cause me harm is unforgivable. You deliberately revealed the circumstances of my birth to society, and encouraged all to remember. My heart is shredded, and I feel as if I have lost *everything*. I feel no hope…only anger and pain." Tumultuous emotions blazed in her green eyes.

Self-loathing filled him. She turned and walked away, but he could only let her go.

I feel no hope…only anger and pain. Those were the last words of Marissa's last letter before she took her life.

Chapter Seventeen

Lucan calculated that he had lain in the same position for almost six hours. Staring at the ceiling, wondering how it had all gone so bloody wrong. How could he have sunken so low as to take his revenge on a young lady that had been as sweet as Marissa? "How do I fix my fool-hardiness," he said softly to the Reverend who had been sitting beside him in silence for the past hour.

The Reverend got up and drew the drapes allowing sunlight inside the library. Lucan cursed, and draped a forearm over his closed eyes. Imbibing so liberally upon his return had been foolish. For the second time in a decade he had gotten drunk. He looked at the bottle of brandy on his oak desk and swore then and there that never would he allow it to happen again.

"So the lady turned from you the minute you confessed what you had done," Ainsley murmured. "I had not expected that, my friend. I can now only beg your forgiveness for what my action has wrought. I was foolishly playing matchmaker."

He ended on a grimace.

Lucan slowly stood and rang the bell. He ordered a pot of tea and some sandwiches to be delivered to the library, then moved across the room and sat behind his desk wondering how much to share with his friends. He observed Ainsley closely. The man did look contrite. His method to get Lucan to recognize his feelings for Constance was unorthodox to say the least, and it would take some time for him to forgive Ainsley the censure he caused society to levy against her.

Lucan grimaced, he was the guiltiest culprit of all. All the pain, anger and hate she felt led directly back to him. "I did not get to confess my shame."

That had both his friends giving him their undivided regard.

"I do not understand," the Reverend said with a frown. "If Lady Constance is not aware of the role you played in her downfall from society why did she reject you, and more importantly, why did you not confess all to her as you had planned?"

Lucan leaned back in his chair, clacking his fingers against the surface of his desk. "I did not confess because the lady was already aware. It is on the basis of my sins she has rebuffed all affections I hold for her and refutes them as lies."

"Good God man," Ainsley rasped. "How did she find out? You have been most discreet."

"It hardly matters now," Lucan said. "I have injured her beyond repair and I do not know how to fix it. What can I do to regain her good opinion?"

"I doubt you ever had her good opinion," the Reverend countered. "She saw you in a romantic light as do all the young ladies of society. For her to so easily discredit your offer of marriage when it is the best thing for her under the circumstances does not speak of a young lady that had affections for you."

Lucan launched to his feet and walked over to the windows. He was silent for a few moments reflecting on Constance. How she laughed, her strength of character despite being faced with such adversities, ones he had wrought. Her passion as she had expressed her contempt for his behavior. Despite having declared her love for him. Despite being so ruined, knowing society would never forgive her, she refused his hand. She refused a duke, when being married to the wealth and status he controlled would have made her sins forgotten. "She reacted as a lady who was wronged," he said to the room at large. "As a woman who had been hurt and betrayed, and I cannot shy away from it or condemn her for it. I must either choose to move on or to fight for her."

"And what will you do?" Ainsley asked as he moved to stand beside him.

"I want her. I realized far too late that the thought of her not in my life…at this time I cannot imagine such a future. Mayhap in time it will fade…"

"So you will fight for her?" Ainsley murmured, sounding pleased.

"I will try my damnedest and the lady still may not have me."

"I do not believe her brothers will allow you close to her for courtship, and if Lady Constance has hardened her heart against you, how will you get the opportunity to soften it?" the Reverend asked.

Lucan was silent, thinking on Constance's words to him.

"I do not believe I will ever be able to convince her of my affections." No, her pain had been too real, too deep.

"But I will give her what she most wants before I depart from her life."

"And that is?" The Revered asked.

"Her place in society where she belongs," Lucan said softly. As he made the vow, it traveled though his mind and heart. He doubted Constance would want him ever again. In fact, he realized it might be best for him to stay away from her. For he would only cause her more pain. But this he would try to give her, in the hopes that one day he might be able to absolve himself of all his sins against her.

• • •

It had been three days since Lucan had seen Constance. The clawing emptiness and regret he felt inside had not abated, and his dreams were filled with images of her devastation.

He had never loved another in a romantic way, though he wondered if the feelings swelling in his chest and roiling in his mind were love. He'd certainly had a few lovers in the past to chase the loneliness away. He had never kept a mistress, and he would never do so. He'd never held any deep attachment to a female outside of his family, but what he felt for Constance was more than warm affection. He loved her.

It damn well hurt, the thought of never seeing her eyes sparkle with delight, of not hearing the throaty chuckle that spilled from her lips whenever she was amused. The idea to never taste her lips or feel her passion again was unbearable. It had been less than a week, and he could only hope the clawing need burgeoning inside of him daily for her presence would eventually fade.

There was a sound, and he turned to see the Dowager Duchess of Ellington strolled into her domain. He admired her cool aplomb. His call on her had been unexpected, and it was not as if they socialized. He had been waiting for almost an hour in the drawing room while she readied to receive him. He had waited with a patience that he himself admired.

Lucan needed someone powerful and influential, someone who commanded the highest respect of the rest of the peerage. Someone he did not own. But someone he could offer something that they needed. That was what drove him to the home of the dowager duchess after making several rounds to those that did owe him.

"Mondvale, to what do I owe this unexpected pleasure?" she drawled as she moved to sit on her chaise. She was clad in a dark blue gown, lined with buttons from her neck down and an elaborate hairstyle which piled her hair high on her head. The lady even had strands of pearls draped across her throat. Lucan now understood why he had waited so long for her to make an appearance.

"It is said you are very skilled at forcing society to accept another, to forgive indiscretions. I require your service," he said without indulging in inane pleasantries.

She stiffened. "Indeed?" cool brown eyes assessed him with something akin to admiration. "Speak, Mondvale."

He walked over and sank onto the sofa directly across from her. "Lady Constance Thornton."

Lucan doubted he needed to say much more.

An elegant brow arched. "You cannot simply require my service and it is given. And from the rumors that are in circulation this was not merely an indiscretion, Your Grace. I encourage people to overlook another's minor indiscretion, this young lady is…" She gave an indelicate shrug as if to indicate he should draw his own conclusion.

"You are correct in your assertions, Lady Ellington. I do not want society to overlook any indiscretion; I want it be known there was *none*. I want her elevated."

She sucked in a harsh breath. "What you ask is impossible, Your Grace."

"You are influential, a member of the Marlborough house set. If anyone can do it, it is you. I want Lady Constance to become the toast of the season."

Lady Ellington's smile broadened. "You are nothing if not ambitious. The young lady is ruined. And if the rumors are to be believed, it was by *your* hand."

"The rumors are not to be believed, and you have the influence to see it done. That is what I require of you, Lady Ellington."

"It will cost you, Your Grace."

He met her gaze, taking her measure. She returned his stare unflinchingly confident in her societal power. He thought of the secrets he knew of her, the ones she thought were carefully hidden. Yet, Lucan hesitated in pursuing such a path. He did not want anything related to Constance to be achieved via blackmail. He knew a few of the scandals the dowager duchess tried to bury, and the amount of debt her son was busy incurring, along with the opium he dabbled in. Lucan had made it his business to know everything about her because she was powerful in the eyes of the *haute monde*. "I will be indebted to you, Lady Ellington, for repayment whenever you desire," he offered.

Surprise chased her features, then she nodded, her eyes calculating. "What is Lady Constance to you that you will try to restore her reputation, after the damning article in the scandal sheets?"

He smiled fleetingly at her audacity. "That, madam, is not your concern. Can you do it?"

Lady Ellington hesitated and his gut tightened. He wanted to keep this clean, so he hoped she would not test his ruthlessness, for she would lose.

"It cannot be me alone that is seen aiding her. Others will be necessary as well. I recommend—"

"You will have the Earl of Blade and his family's full support. Lady Prescott will also be at your disposal. I require utmost discretion."

"I would also recommend Lady Vivian Ashford."

Lucan frowned, thinking of what he knew of Lady Ashford. She had not made it into his black book at all. He only dealt with those he held secrets about. Before he could question her the dowager duchess expounded.

"Several years ago Lady Ashford was known as The Paragon. She helped me at one time with a delicate issue I had, and she was very efficient. She moves within society, smoothing out scandals and stopping gossip where needed. It would be good to have her on your side, if you wish to succeed."

He nodded. "It will be done."

Lady Ellington smiled at his arrogance. "If I have your permission I will speak with Lady Ashford. She is no longer referred to as The Paragon, but she is very gracious and is influential in many circles. While I do not believe you will need to offer Lady Ashford any compensation for her aid, it would be wonderful, however, to let it be known that the Duke of Mondvale will be available if she ever needs your assistance."

"You have my permission."

The speculation grew in her gaze, and then a slow smile of admiration lifted her lips. "I see. I will make my rounds in the morning, Your Grace."

He stood and sketched a small bow. "It is very important, Lady Ellington, that it is understood that any words or actions that threatens Lady Constance's happiness, that any hints of her illegitimacy, will meet with unimaginable consequences."

"I see," Lady Ellington murmured. "Should I indicate a wedding soon? An alliance between Calydon and Mondvale."

He willed his body to relax. "No. Our names must not be linked under any circumstances while you move through society. In fact, it is best you paint me as unworthy of Lady Constance as subtly and delicately as possible."

Lady Ellington rose to her feet and dipped in a shallow curtsy. "I understand, Mondvale."

He titled his head in acknowledgment and walked away. This was just the beginning of his atonement.

The hardest thing would be facing Constance again.

Chapter Eighteen

Over the course of three weeks, the whispers around Constance had started to change. Her moniker evolved from her being the *Beautiful Bastard* to *the Untouchable One*. Young men and titled lords who had before ignored her, afraid of tainting their names, now became intrigued.

Invitations to balls and soirees arrived in tidal waves from the same people who had not long ago shunned her as undesirable. At first she had been skeptical, but she had accepted a few invitations and had been stunned at her reception. She was received with the greatest of cordiality by Lady Blade, whose musicale Constance attended. The countess and her daughter Lady Elisabeth had made every effort to converse and entertain her. Their efforts had been remarked upon on several occasions, before a few of society's matrons had found one matter or another to comment to Constance.

Callers had been slower, but they had presented themselves

to Lord Radcliffe's townhouse all smiles and charming grace. A few young men had tried to invite her on carriage rides, but she rejected them all. Lord Litchfield proposed once again and she refused him as gently as possible, to his outrage. He had gotten a bit nasty, referring to her as soiled goods. His profuse apology a few seconds later had fallen on deaf ears, and she had not seen him since.

Her most surprising callers had been influential ladies of the *haute monde*, more acquainted with her mother than herself. The only lady that had seemed genuine and caring had been the beautiful Lady Ashford. She had been so warm and sincere, and within a few minutes Constance had relaxed with her. Constance had even dined at Lady Ashford's London home, where she met Lady Ashford's dashing and somewhat roguish husband and their children. At first, Constance had been apprehensive, but the earl had charmed her, especially with his vivid and gripping tales of his adventures in Africa.

She had then attended Lady Prescott's soirée only at Jocelyn, Phillipa, and Lady Ashford's encouragement, and it was there she noted that the whispers had faded. The first young man to have requested her hand for a dance had been severely embarrassed by her rejection. It had not been intentional for her to walk away without responding. Her shock had been simply too great. Constance had, of course realized, what was happening. Someone was influencing her acceptance into society, but the joy of being received so well meant nothing to her. It had been a startling admission to realize the folds she would have desperately wanted to be accepted into a few months ago, were now inconsequential. She had no interest in men, especially those now seemed eager to court her.

Sebastian and Anthony noted the shift, had even mentioned they believed Lucan had something to do with it. Her breath had caught, and she had worked to hide all emotions at that declaration. Despite the pain that lingered in her heart, she missed him fiercely. But it was the dreams that tormented her. Wildly inappropriate dreams of her splayed open to him, while he poured champagne over her skin and licked her. *Everywhere.* She would awaken in shambles of twisted need, between her legs throbbing in a desperation she did not understand. Constance only knew she ached for him, that in the nights when everyone slept, she wept for what they could have been.

"Constance." The warm tones of her mother had her closing the volume she had been reading.

"Yes, Mother?"

"You have a personal invitation."

Her mother handed her a peach vellum paper with Constance's name elegantly scrawled across its back. She reached for the letter opener and slit the seal, curious as to its content. She read it in silence, her heart thumping.

"What is it my dear?"

"It is an invitation to Lady Ellington's annual ball." The dowager duchess of Ellington's invitation was most sought after.

Constance gave it to her mother who scanned the short but very personalized invitation, before handing it back to her.

"Would you like to attend?" her mother asked as her usual wont for all invitations they received of late.

Constance felt very ambivalent about it. Her mother showed some excitement, and Constance had to remind herself she was not the only party affected. While Lucan had ensured most of society's scorn was directed at her, her mother had been affected as well. Her hand trembled, and she clenched the invitation in her hands. When would it abate? The pain that came whenever Constance thought about all she had endured and the knowledge that the man who had kissed and touched her so intimately was the same one who had encouraged society to shred her. She pushed the bitter thoughts from her mind and smiled in what she hoped was an excited manner. "Yes, I believe I will."

Her mother nodded in approval and sipped her lemonade. "I believe it would be wise, my dear, to accept a few dance partners at this one. Even if it is only Lord Litchfield."

"No," Constance said firmly. On that she would not budge. While she did not rebel against society for seeking to forgive her perceived infractions, she had not forgiven them as readily as her mother.

"Constance," her mother said with an exasperated sigh. "You must not behave foolishly. I have heard several young men referring to you as the Untouchable One, and in admiring tones. I need not remind you how swiftly the tide of society's opinion can change. Lord Litchfield has tried at least twice this week to walk with you in the park, and you have refused him. He is an exceedingly agreeable man. With a good fortune and connections and I can see you having a good life with him."

"I do not care about society's opinion nor for the regard of Lord Litchfield."

"Then what *do* you care about?" her mother snapped, slamming the glass of lemonade on the center table. "Sebastian has secured a bevy of invitations for you this week, and you have rejected them *all*. You have pleaded with him to not secure an invitation for you to the Prince of Wales' annual country house party. This indifference you display cannot continue."

Constance closed her eyes and gathered her composure. "I care about purchasing winter clothes and supplies for the home Mr. and Mrs. Benton operates. I care about hiring a tutor to help them educate the unwanted children they so generously care for. Not balls, not riding, and not picnics, and certainly not suitors. And most of all, I care about Charlotte, mother. My only friend that you thought to dismiss from my life despite my pleas." *And Lucan, I care about Lucan.*

Her mother had the grace to blush and look discomfited. At every opportunity Constance inserted her anger at her mother's actions against Charlotte.

"She endangered you. I could no longer, in good conscience, have her remain employed here. Your father agreed."

Constance closed her eyes in frustration lest she screamed. "Charlotte did not endanger me mother. She acted as a true and caring friend by willingly following me into the club. I had been determined, and she understood. Instead you punished her for it. That is what I care about, the well-being of my friend. She needed this job, and you terminated her without any reference."

She had argued with her mother on several occasions, ever since she received Charlotte's note informing her that she was considering becoming the mistress of Marcus Stone. *His mistress*. Charlotte had not divulged the circumstances that led her to entering such an arrangement no matter how Constance had inquired. She had promised to send money and sell her diamonds if Charlotte needed, but her friend had refused. Constance had never felt so helpless. But she was soothed by Charlotte's daily letters, which indicated she was at least safe, and she even seemed happy.

"Please excuse me, Mother. I have a bit of headache, and I need some fresh air." Constance rose and exited the parlor, heading for the entrance that led to the gardens. Charlotte had encouraged her to travel with Anthony and Phillipa on their grand tour, and Constance had been in firm agreement. There was nothing for her in England, and she badly needed space to heal and forget Lucan. She only prayed with distance the tormenting dreams that left her so needy would dissipate, and she could move on with her life.

. . .

Lady Ellington's annual ball was a crushing success. Lucan stepped out tonight for the first time in weeks, wanting to observe Constance's reception for himself. He had been careful to ensure he was not seen at the same social gathering as her over the past few weeks, not wanting their names to be linked. After only being inside the glittering ballroom for a few minutes, the soft whispers of voices referring to her as the Untouchable One reached his ears and infuriated him. He drifted through the crowd, skillfully staying in the background listening. While he was angry at her new moniker, he felt pleased with the other whispers he heard from Lady Prescott to a group of other high society ladies lounging by the refreshment table.

"Lady Constance is a most extraordinary young lady. In character and in her mind. So elegant and well poised," Lady Prescott murmured.

"Indeed," the Countess of Blade affirmed. "I have

always thought her well-mannered and intelligent."

Lucan made a note to forgive Lord Prescott his debt at *Decadence*, and to gift Lady Blade's daughters horses sired from his much coveted thoroughbred champions. Heat rippled over his skin, and instinct had him slipping behind a column as he discreetly scanned the crowed room. When he spied Constance, need drove the air from his lungs. Draped in a silver gown, low cut enough where he could see the swell of her breasts, the lady looked exquisite. Floral designs embroidered the hems of her dress and sleeves, and similarly in her hair that was plaited to appear like a crown on her head, and rubies dripped from her ears and throat. She was oblivious to the many admiring and envious stares of young ladies and gentlemen. In fact, the look on her face was sheer boredom.

"Beautiful isn't she?" an intense voice asked from beside him.

Lucan glanced at the Viscount of Belfry, trying to ignore the flare of hot jealously that filled him at the look of hunger in the man's eyes. But Lucan needed to do better in masking his emotions. The only reason Belfry could possibly have to mention Constance was because he must have seen the naked desire Lucan stared at her with. He needed to be more discreet, but to look at her without being able to touch her hurt.

"She is," he agreed, forcing his limbs to relax.

The man gave him a probing look, and Lucan could see the knowledge of the rumors in Belfry's eyes. Lucan could also see the speculation.

"Lady Constance has yet to favor any man with a dance, perhaps she is waiting for a request from you," Belfry insinuated slyly.

Lucan forced himself to chuckle disarmingly, very much aware of the way several ladies and lords were suddenly attentive and trying not to be obvious. A few even had the temerity to step closer. "I have tried, but the lady refused me. Said I am not fit to lick her shoes," Lucan drawled.

Everyone went quiet and a young lady gasped.

"And as she should," a hushed voice carried to him. "He is a libertine. I always said she was a young lady of good sense."

"A very *rich* libertine with a dukedom. A fine catch I would say," another voice rebuffed. "But it is evident she is a young lady of good sense, despite circumstances that were certainly not her fault."

Lucan's lips curled in disgust. This was what he wanted, opinions of her shifted, but society was all too fickle. He walked toward the terrace and was surprised to see Belfry ambling beside him.

"Then you have no intentions toward the lady?" Belfry asked.

The look he dealt the man had Belfry tugging at his cravat in agitation.

"I meant honorable intentions," he muttered, face scrunched in discomfort. "I mean no dishonor to Lady Constance, Mondvale. I merely wondered if the lady is free for a twirl in the garden," Lord Belfry said.

Lucan smiled. "You may have better luck than everyone else. The lady is generous, I am sure she will afford you a dance."

Belfry nodded eagerly and strolled over to Constance.

Lucan discreetly watched as she spurned the advance of the fifth man to seek her hand in a dance. She gave Belfry a vacant smile and after a few seconds the man departed, his face flushed in obvious embarrassment. What was the minx doing? Was not this what she wanted? She had railed at him that she had no friends, saying he had torn her from all she held dear, so why was she not basking in her restoration? Lucan needed her to be happy. He needed to know that he had brought good into her life, more than he needed his next breath.

He slipped onto the terrace, keeping her in his line of sight. She had yet to see him and he wanted it kept that way. Ainsley stepped from the shadows and walked over to him, and they stood in silence watching her reject partner after partner.

"What the hell is she doing?" Lucan growled in frustration, though he felt a deep sense of admiration in her actions.

"In the last three weeks Lady Constance has received over two dozen invitations to balls and picnics. She has attended only four events. The Countess of Fairclough sent an invitation to her daughter's debut ball, and Lady Constance said no," Ainsley informed him.

Lucan gritted his teeth. Why wasn't she blasted heading out? He had been working so hard, pulling in favors to turn the tide against her and it was all for naught? "Is she doing well otherwise?"

As a favor to him Ainsley had attended each event as a guardian. Watching her from the shadows and reporting to Lucan his perception of how she was being received. Ainsley also served to smooth out any negative talk Lady Ashford and the Dowager Duchess had not reached.

Ainsley sighed and raked a hand through his hair. "You could go and visit her, Lucan, invite her to ride out with you. Better yet, she is standing right across from us. Go ask her to dance. She may be tempted to accept you," Ainsley suggested.

Lucan glanced at him wondering if he jested, but his friend's mien was contemplative. "I am sure you jest."

Ainsley raised his brow. "You have not been sleeping or eating. You have forgiven debts of thousands of pounds. You gave Lord Prescott back his twenty thousand pounds and that very beautiful estate in Essex for a simple invitation to his lady's annual ball. The invitation could have been secured for far less, I wager."

Lucan went silent. "It is not time to approach her as yet."

Ainsley laughed mockingly. "We know time waits on no man."

Lucan went cold, knowing Ainsley referred to the painful experience of losing his lady. Lucan tensed as Constance suddenly stiffened. She tilted her head and stared directly at him. It was impossible for her see him, but then he recalled her passionate assurances that she could always feel his gaze upon her. Heated awareness rippled over his skin, Ainsley's presence faded, and all Lucan could see was Constance. Her eyes widened, and a flush of color climbed her cheeks. She took an instinctive step toward him, then grounded to a halt. Her hands visibly trembled, she pressed a palm to her stomach and inhaled deeply. Her eyes darkened with roiling emotions, daring him to approach her.

Lucan's heart jerked a painful cadence in his chest, and he found himself moving across the terrace floor, closer to her, unable to suppress the desire to just be nearer. He stopped shy of entering the ballroom, cocooned in the shadows. They stared at each other for what seemed like endless moments. It pained Lucan to see the unguarded delight glittering in her emerald gaze slowly dampened, before her expression shuttered. Her lashes lowered, and she subtly shifted away, halting the need urging him to walk over to her. A soft breath escaped his lips. No…it was definitely not the time to approach her, especially with Society's watchful eyes still upon her.

Ainsley came up beside him. "When will you go to her and plead your case?"

To her? The pleasure that had warmed her eyes upon seeing him filled Lucan with hope, but he'd also espied the flash of raw agony, and the strength of her continued pain sliced deep. She needed more time. But to her family… He clenched his teeth as he faced what he should have done weeks ago, but had been delaying. "I have an appointment to see Calydon tomorrow."

"Hell!"

Lucan understood Ainsley's sentiment. In all his plotting, he never imagined he would be visiting Calydon under such circumstances. Calydon had stepped into *Decadence* the week before and Lucan had fought off the primitive wave of satisfaction that had filled him. Instead of forcing the confrontation he had plotted for so many months, Lucan had ducked out, shocking himself. It was then he had understood the depth of how much Constance meant to him. He had drawn on his coat and hat, collected his cane, escaped the building, and walked toward the Thames, watching the subtle currents that ran in the water. That was when he had realized he had abandoned all revenge against Calydon. Albeit too late. To have Constance in his life, he must do so with a clean slate, a heart clean of vengeance. And suddenly it had been easy. There had been no fight, no regret, just hope that she would forgive him for hurting her. And he would be able to claim the woman he had come to love.

Chapter Nineteen

The silence in Calydon's library was a cold one, yet it had not discomfited Lucan. The man had expected Lucan, and he had been received with civility. Calydon's duchess had floated in only a few seconds after Lucan was given entrance to the library, obviously pregnant and clearly hoping to make the tension that now seethed in the air less somehow. Lucan feared she failed abysmally. Calydon indicated she should wait in the drawing room, and she had only muttered "nonsense" with a smile and taken a seat.

Tension roiled in the air, and Lucan had been picturing Constance's face for the past few minutes to thaw the icy rage that had flared inside and encased him upon seeing the man. Calydon roused Lucan's ire instead of forgiving thoughts. Constance needed him to be forgiving, to be understanding. But it pained him to see Calydon standing in such wealth, experiencing such happiness and love with his duchess while Marissa *rotted*, beyond redemption, her soul lost and tormented if Lucan was to believe the church.

Lady Calydon's dark beauty was quite stunning, and so was the apparent control her presence had on the duke. It was as if she grounded him and prevented him from attacking Lucan. A smile twisted his lips, and he fancied it was unpleasant from Lady Calydon's blanch.

"Are you here to offer for Constance?" Calydon asked from where he stood by the windows. The man did not even face him.

"No," Lucan said flatly.

The man turned with affected calm, but Lucan could see the controlled violence Calydon emitted.

"Why not?" The strident demand came from Lady Calydon. She shifted in the high wing-back chair she sat in, and rested her hand with tender care on her rounded stomach. Her gray eyes as she assessed Lucan were actually welcoming, which he found quite strange.

"I am here to lay the demons that haunt me to rest, nothing more." He had no plans to get ahead of himself. This was just one hurdle he had to cross. After he had secured Constance's forgiveness he would approach Calydon for her hand.

"Marissa," the duke murmured.

"Yes."

Pain flared deep in Calydon's gaze before he lowered his lashes, obscuring his eyes. "I never knew Marissa had a brother."

Lucan flinched. No, he doubted she would have been proud to talk of her merchant connections. Not when she had aspired to move in loftier circles. "Is that why you thought nothing of treating her with such callous disregard?" he asked softly. "Because she had no one to defend her honor?"

Calydon thrust his hands in the pocket of his trousers and met Lucan's gaze without blinking.

"I met Marissa when I was young," Calydon said bluntly. "I was enchanted by her, though I knew I did not want a wife. You see, I was very turned away from the notion of marriage, and thought no woman would honor their marriage vows. I am now aware of how misguided I was."

Lucan stared at the man. This was Calydon's defense? He had not wanted a wife? "Yet you took Marissa's purity and ruined her for marriage," Lucan snarled.

Calydon grimaced. "We courted and danced around each other for a couple years...then I did take her innocence. And I did battle with offering for her afterwards. She knew how I felt about marriage, but after a few weeks I realized none of it mattered. For I loved her."

"Love?" Lucan demanded the rage he was trying to fight firing to life.

"Yes, I loved her. What was later revealed as a bid to force my hand, Marissa accepted an offer from Lord Stanhope. I was young and foolish and saw it as a betrayal, despite dragging my feet to offer for her. I went to explain my initial reluctance and to ask for her hand when I saw her with him, making love. It was hard for me to reconcile her being intimate with someone that was not me. We argued and it became evident that she had been intimate with both of us from the very beginning. When she perceived she had lost a duke, she went for an earl."

Lucan closed his eyes and turned away. Calydon told him nothing he did not know, but it was still painful to hear. It made it all the more real.

"I do not intend to malign your sister. I am simple

presenting the facts as how they were for me." Calydon's voice was sincere. "I went away for a few months, and when I returned she was the Countess of Stanhope. It did not take long for us to resume our affair…and it lasted for years."

"I know," Lucan said.

Lady Calydon stiffened. "I don't understand, if you knew, why you did—"

She flushed at the look he dealt her.

"I knew all from the moment Marissa met and fell in love with Calydon. We were close. I was her rock and she my joy. She wrote to me, and wherever I was her letters found me. Sometimes months later. But I knew every thought, every hope and dream she had in relation to you, Calydon. I know how flawed and imperfect she was. I know of her continued affair with you after marrying, I know of the brutal beatings she suffered. I know you claimed you loved her, but abandoned her to the cruelty of a jealous and possessive husband, the scorn of society, I know it broke her, and when she could bear it no more, instead of waiting for me, she took her life."

The duchess rose and went over to Calydon. He wrapped her in his arms and Lucan could see the torment in the man's eyes. "Marissa lied to me…mayhap to you, Mondvale. I wish not to shatter any belief you had in her, but Lord Stanhope had not been beating her. When she accused him, telling me of how he abused her I confronted him. He was eager to fight with me because he knew I was bedding his wife, and I was just as eager because I thought he was her tormentor. I almost killed him. I broke his bones and stripped his pride that day, all on a *lie*." Calydon's hand went to the rapier scar that flayed his left cheek. "And Stanhope gave me this. It was as he lay cursing I realized Stanhope thought I was the one abusing his Marissa. She inflicted the bruises herself. When I confronted her, she urged me to kill him so we could wed. I said no, and ended our association. A few days later she killed herself," he ended on a hoarse note.

The depth of fury surging through Lucan rendered him speechless for a few seconds. "You fucking liar," he snarled.

Lady Calydon jerked as if she had been slapped, and her eyes widened.

He took a step toward Calydon. "Marissa had not been self-inflicting her bruises. You think I did not corroborate her assertions with the servants? Stanhope beat her brutally for days before and after you and he fought. She did not lie to me. She is dead. Because of *your* actions."

Calydon paled, disbelief dawning across his features. "It cannot be so. Marissa confessed—"

"You ruined my most cherished sister, and you stand here and defile her memory with such vicious lies? So I may think you are not as culpable?" The need for violence tore through Lucan and his resolve to forgive Calydon trembled.

Lady Calydon stiffened and her eyes flashed. "My husband did not *ruin* your sister, Mondvale. Sebastian and Marissa were both young and foolish, but my husband did not force ruin upon her. Yet you try to condemn him after you have hurt Constance in the most abominable way? Yes, we are aware you were the one to reveal her circumstances to society, and we are aware you must have only courted her to hurt her. It is *your* actions that are unforgivable, for Connie is innocent in all of this." Lady Calydon's chest heaved and she visibly shook, her gray eyes brewing with rage.

Lucan was unmoved. In fact, she stoked his anger with her defense of Calydon. As if the matter of his sister's death was inconsequential. The crack in his resolve widened, and Lucan battled against the pain closing in on him. Where was the remorse for Calydon's actions toward Marissa?

"I easily condemned your husband because he abandoned Marissa." Lucan's eyes bored into Calydon's. "She was good enough for you to rut with, but not to understand. You did not care enough to delve deep inside and see the scared, lonely woman. She was only a means to you, Calydon. A means for pleasure. Her husband had been abusing her. Marissa would never have lied to me about that. *Never*. She came to you in her despair and instead of protecting her, you abandoned her though you had been her lover for years. I find your actions insupportable. She was not just a mistress, she was *my* most beloved sister. And we both failed her," Lucan said into the painful silence that gripped the library.

He felt shattered. He had never admitted feelings of his own failure to anyone. They had boiled in him for months. His failure of providing enough for her, of being there for her when she needed him. If he had been at home, instead of seeking wealth, she would have been alive. If he had sought the connection he sensed his mother had hidden, he would have found the previous duke of Mondvale and Marissa would have been alive. But these were recriminations he had been over so many times, and dragging them up did not change the situation that Constance had been injured by his anger.

Calydon's voice was regretful, "I was young and stupid, but I was in love with Marissa. My parents' disaster of a marriage had given me a very poor opinion of the state. I saw Marissa's infidelity as proof her feelings had not gone deep. I assure you when we were involved she was not being abused. When she demanded I kill Stanhope, she seemed so unhinged I could no longer see in her the woman I had fallen in love with. She was like a mad thing."

"Yet you abandoned her," Lucan snarled. He jerked back and started to pace the library. The confines of the walls pressed in on him. *Murder?* He could not credit it. But he knew Marissa had been desperate. Her letters had been infused with hopelessness, begging him to return and remove her from Stanhope's clutches. The pain of what she must have suffered almost felled Lucan in that moment.

Calydon rubbed a hand over his face. "Many times I have wondered if I had returned to Marissa, even as a friend, whether she would have come to her senses and things might have turned out differently," Calydon said at Lucan's silence.

He glanced at the man, and he was not sure what Calydon saw in his face, but he tugged his duchess to him and whispered something to her. Lady Calydon gave Lucan a fulminating glare, then with a regal tilt of her head walked out the door.

He could not dismiss the possibility that Calydon was telling the truth. His sister had always been changeable, so he could almost put himself in Calydon's place and understand why he had turned away. *Murder?* The circumstance would have been shocking to anyone. For the first time Lucan wondered whether even if he had been in England, would his presence have made any difference to the tragic ending of Marissa's life? He had argued with her so much via letters to end her affair with Calydon. Lucan had given her wealth and had worked hard to ensure she was situated financially, and she had still been unhappy.

The door closed softly on Lady Calydon's exit, and the veneer of civility Calydon had been showing stripped away.

The man advanced on Lucan and cold satisfaction settled in his gut. He did not resist when Calydon jerked him by the lapel of his jacket and pushed him against the wall with controlled violence. Lucan smiled and welcomed the icy rage bleeding into his veins. The pain roiling in him needed an outlet. He wanted to howl, to fight, to do anything to stop the torment of imagining how his sister must have despaired.

"I cannot express the sorrow I have lived with for years in regards to Marissa. When she was happy she was such a radiant thing, but when things did not go exactly as she wished she could be destructive. I knew that, but never did I dream Stanhope would really start beating her. Nor did I ever imagine Marissa would take her life. It gutted me, and I eschewed all female companionship until I met my Duchess years later," Calydon growled. "I deserved your anger. I deserved you trying to damage my business investments, and I assure you Mondvale, you have had some success. But what you have done to Constance is unforgivable. You hurt her. *My* cherished sister, when she was innocent in all of this. The harm you have caused her and Anthony is enough so that I promise I will *ruin* you."

The ruthlessness Lucan had only read about glared from Calydon's blue eyes. They were so cold, Lucan thought it was a wonder Calydon's teeth did not clatter. Lucan creased his lips in a cruel smile, pain and rage edging him. He gripped Calydon's hand where it crushed his jacket and pushed from the wall, standing toe to toe with him.

"It is not a pleasant thought is it, Calydon?" Lucan taunted, a deeper coldness encasing his heart. "What kind of thoughts filled when you thought I *fucked* your sister and abandoned her to the cruel fates of society? Did you not hear the whispers that taunted my sister? 'Marissa the Used,' 'Marissa the Abandoned.'"

Speaking of Constance in such a crude manner left a vile taste in Lucan's mouth, but something raw in him demanded that some of the hatred, some of the pain he had lived with for years be felt by Calydon.

Calydon stilled rage lighting his eyes, then doubt.

"Is Connie untouched?" he demanded.

Lucan's slow smile was deliberately sensual, remembering how he had touched Constance and letting the knowledge seeped into his eyes.

He was impressed with how intimidating Calydon suddenly appeared. If Lucan was a lesser man he would have been quaking in his boots. In fact, he was doing everything in his power to resist smashing his fist in the man's face. Lucan could see the dark need in Calydon to offer him violence as well. Probably Lucan had underestimated the effect of the duchess' presence. Without her, Calydon had no need to still the roiling rage inside of himself.

Calydon dropped his hand, and Lucan saw the fist coming. He could have dodged it. Hell, he could possibly have had Calydon on the ground before the man realized what was happening. But Lucan deserved it. Constance was all that was pure and lovely, and should never play any part in his vengeance again.

Lucan's head snapped back from the force of the punch, it rocked him back on his heels. He raised his hand and wiped the thin trickle of blood from the corner of his mouth. "I deserved that, for Constance does not merit my vulgarity or insinuations. But I assure you it will be the only free hit you get, Calydon."

Calydon's eyes narrowed. "If you had thought to ask for

her hand, it is denied. The only reason I am not ripping into you is because I know how tirelessly you have been working for society to welcome her back into their folds. That is the only reason, Mondvale."

A hollow sensation formed in the pit of Lucan's stomach and he dismissed it. "Your threat is irrelevant. Lady Constance will not have me." At least not yet, but he would do everything in his power to have her fall back in love with him. Lucan was resolved, for he could accept no other outcome. Living without her smiles and kisses have been too bleak.

Calydon's eyes remained hard and unforgiving. Lucan fully understood.

"You proposed to her?" Calydon demanded.

Lucan thrust his hands in his pockets. "I did," he answered. "Constance rejected me."

"Connie has not mentioned this," Calydon said, surprise evident in his tone.

Lucan raised a brow. "It is not for me to speculate why Lady Constance felt she could not confide in her own brother."

Calydon stiffened, but Lucan ignored him.

"I doubt you and I will ever be friends," Lucan said. "But I have considered how young you and Marissa both were. My intention today was not to force any confrontation." His mouth twisted in a wry grimace. "I had only intended to lay what haunts me to rest so I can relinquish all need in my heart for vengeance."

Calydon face was devoid of all expression, but Lucan knew he listened keenly.

"I confess I hurt Constance in the cruelest of fashion. I did start out to ruin her, but I couldn't. She is enchanting, kind, everything I could ever want in a lady. In *my lady*. If you want satisfaction for the hurt I have caused her, you will have it."

He noted the surprise that flashed in Calydon's gaze before he masked it.

"I've destroyed Constance's love for me, and I don't know if I can ever get it back. I saw her at Lady Ellington's Ball, and although she is now welcomed in society, I could still see that she is shattered. I am tormented day and night, and I need to know that she is happy, for I love her. I am also declaring my intention to eventually court her, for whether you want to hear it or not, I love your sister, more than I thought possible to love another." Lucan admitted frankly.

"Deluded, but not so jaded and hard hearted," Calydon murmured a smile curving his lips.

Lucan looked at the man blankly. What the hell was he blathering about?

"I wager it will take a while for us to be civil to each other," Calydon offered. "I can imagine the hatred you must feel, and I even accept it. For I wanted to crush you when I saw Connie's pain, and she had not suffered as Marissa. So I understand some of your pain if not fully. And I hope you can eventually forgive me for the part I played in Marissa's hurt…and I will endeavor to forgive your role in Connie's pain."

Lucan nodded, the acknowledgment soothing the edge of rage that still lingered. Though he only had to think of Constance, and it all deflated. He stood in silence as he remembered the vibrant woman Marissa had been in her happy days. He pushed it from his mind for he had vowed to forgive, to understand and to learn.

"I suggest we make use of my sparring room. From all accounts you are an excellent fighter, and I think it is time we went into the ring together," Calydon mused. "Then when we pound on each other, the excuse I can give my duchess is that we were simply sparring."

Lucan watched as Calydon went to the mantel and poured brandy into two glasses. Lucan accepted when Calydon held one out to him.

"Constance?" Lucan asked. He had been battling the need to show his weakness for her, but then decided it did not matter. What objections would he face when he tried to court her?

"I believe you love Constance. But you will have to wait until she has returned to England to pay your address. I will not force her where her heart does not lie. Though I believe it belongs to you."

Nothing the man said made an impact on Lucan. He was stuck on Constance not being in England. "Constance is not in the country?" he demanded.

A cool smile curved Calydon's lips. "No. She boarded a train this morning with Anthony and Phillipa for Europe. They may then move onto Egypt."

A crushing weight descended on Lucan's chest. "How long?" At Calydon's silence, Lucan went cold. "How long will she be gone for?" he repeated.

"A year."

His stomach hollowed out. *A year?* A year in which she may meet someone else, be wooed and fall in love?

"Tell me where she is."

"No." Calydon's voice was implacable. "She is *my* most cherished sister, and if she needs this, I will give it to her. I know love, and I understand the need I can see blazing from you to go to her. But in this, I will not have her thwarted."

Lucan inclined his head, then spun and walked away. He would not plead; he could see the man was unbending. He would hire men to find her. But he realized it would mean nothing. He had waited too long, he had been foolish, and now the emptiness he felt was profound.

He had lost her.

Chapter Twenty

Lady Constance has returned to Sherring Cross.
You have my blessings if she will have you.
        Calydon

Lucan's heart slammed into his throat. He read the note for the second time hardly daring to breathe, to hope. Constance had returned after only three months. He knew it may not have anything to do with him, but hope hot and sweet poured through him. Did this mean Calydon had somehow delivered Lucan's letter to her? When he had realized he would be without her for a year, or longer, or possibly forever, he had poured everything into a letter and asked Calydon to see it delivered to wherever she traveled.

You have my blessings if she will have you.

Lucan understood full well the honor Calydon accorded him after he had tried to ruin his sister. The man was forgiving. Damn well more forgiving than Lucan himself would have been. But then, Calydon had looked Lucan directly in the eyes and vowed to destroy him if he ever hurt his Connie again. He had believed the man, though the warning had not been necessary. If she would give him a chance, he would love and treasure her with every breath in his body.

He hoped the fact that Calydon had given his blessings, indicated a change of heart on the lady's part. While Lucan and Calydon had formed some sort of tentative friendship, the man had never once hinted where Constance had traveled to, no matter how often Lucan had demanded. He had wanted to travel the oceans, follow her to wherever she traveled and convince her to marry him. These past three months had been agony for him, where he envisioned several scenarios of the men he had scouring the continent for her, finding her, and giving him her location. He would then kidnap her and take her to his castle in Scotland where he would make love to her for days until she agreed to be his wife. But they had only been dreams, while he had waited for the year to draw to an end.

He glanced at the note a final time and then launched into motion, exiting the library where he had been ensconced for the long morning dealing with several business matters, namely the restoration of his entailed estates. He ordered his carriage around and for his bags to be packed, and sent out several missives alerting his friends to where he traveled, for it would take him a couple of days to reach Sherring Cross to see her.

Lucan prayed like he had never done before.

He prayed Constance returning was a sign in the lessening of her anger.

He prayed it meant she would forgive him. That she still

loved him.

And he prayed he would have the strength to let her go if she did not want him.

Because Calydon would hunt him to the end of the earth if Lucan executed his plans of kidnapping her and secluding her at his castle until she married him. He smiled, though it was without humor, for he was fully aware, he would do anything to bind his green-eyed bewitching beauty to his side.

"Your Grace."

He paused in the act of climbing the final steps of the mansion's winding stairs and looked down at his butler. "What is it, Alfred?"

"There is a young lady here to see you."

Lucan glanced toward the parlor, not wanting any delay in his leaving. "Lady Penelope?" he asked drily. Since his retirement to Wynter Park, his ducal estate these past weeks, the young lady tended to travel miles to visit him. She and her mother, the Viscountess of Fordham. It seemed the ambitious mammas of the *haute monde* were everywhere. He had not the withal to entertain them today.

"No, Your Grace, and this young lady is in the gardens. She said to tell you she is waiting for you. She refused to leave a name, Your Grace." The butler sounded disgruntled and bemused at the same time.

"She refused to identify herself?" Lucan did not have time for foolish games. "And you did not refuse entry?" he demanded.

Alfred flushed. "Though petite, the lady has the will of—"

"Petite?" Lucan demanded a little too forcefully. For a split second, he felt as if he had been stabbed through the chest and his knees went weak. It couldn't be her.

"Where exactly is she?" His estate was large with several gardens and lakes.

"She is by the rose gardens, Your Grace, I—"

He bounded down the stairs two at a time, passed the startled Alfred, and ran into the gardens. Lucan's heart thudded and he forced his mind to be quiet. It could be anyone, but God, he knew.

He broke into a sprint after he couldn't stand the suspense any longer. He slowed to a stroll as he neared and entered the secluded gardens as quietly as he could. A lady sat on a stone bench, spine taut, her back to him, dressed in a black crepe that covered her from head to toe. He saw the flash of her hands and a letter in them.

His letter.

The raw fear that filled him was unwelcomed. She was here to give him her answer, a yea or a nay. He held his breath in an agony of anticipation willing her to *feel* him, to face him.

• • •

Dear Constance,

My very first memory was seeing my sister Marissa take her first halting step. I had not thought to start this letter in such a manner, but the depth of affection and love I felt for my sister dictated much of my life and subsequent actions. It is not an excuse for the unforgivable way I have treated you. But I hope that in reading my words, you can find it in you to forgive me for hurting you.

Marissa had flaws and I own to them. They were flaws that allowed her to behave recklessly and hurt others with her selfish desires. She was also a warm, caring, and beautiful young lady, a most beloved and cherished sister. We grew up believing we had no ties to nobility or anything to recommend us to the life Marissa craved. When we lost our parents, I became her rock, and she was my solace in the enduring hardship I faced in working and living in London. I was in the Americas when I came into the possession of her last letter. She swore to end her life after being rejected by everyone she thought loved her, after being cruelly abused by her husband. I cannot express how my heart broke in that moment knowing she must already be dead, knowing how much she must have suffered and I had not been there. I traveled to London post-haste to discover she had already been dead and buried for several months. I will not burden you with the sordid details, but I am sure you know by now Marissa had been Calydon's mistress before and after she was married. I see now they were both misguided, reckless and more than foolhardy in their passion for each other. But before I reached this opinion, I vowed to destroy everyone that played a part in her tragic death. It was the only way I felt I could repay her for not being there when she needed me. It was with this thought sustaining me that I directed my attentions to you when I realized Calydon also had a sister he cherished. I thought to repay hurt with hurt and pain with pain. But I was wrong.

From the moment I met you, you captivated me body and soul. Your beauty, your kind and generous mannerisms, even your scent stirred and enraptured me. When I realized my feelings for you were interfering with my vengeance, I tried to push you away. In the end, an end that may be too late for us, I now know you are more important to me than anything else.

When you return to London, I will be waiting for you. If you find it in your heart to forgive the pain I have caused you, I ask you to put me out of my misery and consent to be my wife. I see us having a most content and fortuitous future together. If not, I will endeavor to not trouble you with my unwanted affections. I await your response.

Lucan

Constance folded Lucan's letter with tender care. Thunder rumbled overhead and a slight chill nipped at her. As rain started to drizzle, she rose and turned to hurry inside the conservatory, for she would not make it into the main house before the deluge. There was a sound of movement, she spun toward it and froze. *Lucan.* Her breath caught, everything seemed still in that moment. She could not move for the feelings washing through her. *He is here.*

He stared at her in silence, his chillingly beautiful eyes piercing as arrows. The profound relief in his gaze had the tension melting from her frame. She had missed him so.

Dressed in dark brown trousers and jacket, a white shirt,

and riding boots, he looked splendid. A drop of rain splashed on her forehead, rolling into her eyes, but she did not blink, fearful that if she did, he would disappear.

He pushed his spectacles firmly onto his nose. His endearingly sweet, nervous gesture.

"I...Lucan, I am here," she said softly. "I received your letter."

His eyes blazed with emotions and raw tension emanated from him. He took a shuddering breath. "Will you have me, Constance?" His voice came out as a low rasp.

No statement of love or a reaffirmation of his earlier proposal, but she knew what he asked. The sky darkened and more rain wetted her. The strong column of his throat convulsed at her silence, and he swallowed. Tenderness pierced her deep at the vulnerability she never imagined she could see in his eyes. She ached to touch him, to hold him, to be held by him.

"Yes," she whispered, but the flare of powerful relief, then desire in his gaze made her aware he heard, even over the distant rumble of thunder. A fork of lightning speared through the sky, a dark cloud blotting out the remainder of the sun, but neither of them moved. Constance felt trapped, weak limbed, yet energized from the need that poured from him, wrapping her in heat, although he did not touch her.

A sob of want and anticipation escaped from her lips as in two strides, he was there drawing her closer. The look on his face caused her pulse to flutter wildly. It was love—stark and agonizing. Yet Lucan's touch as he cradled her face was gentle. He kissed her lips, the corner of her mouth, and then her eyelids with tenderness. "I missed you," he said with aching gentleness. "Your laugh, your taste, your scent, even the fire that snaps into your eyes when you are angry." His hands tightened on her cheeks. "I cannot exist without your forgiveness. To know I have caused you such pain torments me."

Her breath caught, and she rested her forehead against his shoulder, inhaling his warm heady scent. And she could not exist without him. Before she had even received his letter she had begged Anthony to return her from Naples. She had needed to get away from the hurt that had ravaged her, as the pain of Lucan's actions had cut unimaginably deep. But as she had journeyed through the vineyards and ruins of Italy with Anthony and Phillipa, she had pictured Lucan with her. As they had dined in moonlit open-air restaurants, she had imagined it had been with him. In the nights she ached for him, dreamed of him. *Every night.* She knew he had tried to atone and restore what he had deliberately shattered, and she respected him for it. The *haute monde* had forgiven her perceived infractions, but Constance had discovered she did not care for their forgiveness, and that it was hers they needed to earn.

In her weeks away, all she had thought about was the pain that must have driven Lucan to act as how he had. She had regretted not caring more about that pain, not understanding what drove him, for she adored him completely.

"Constance?" The raw uncertainty in his voice had her lifting her head.

A soft smile curved her lips. "You have *all* of me Lucan. My forgiveness, my — "

He took her lips in a primal kiss. Crushing her to him, his lips roved over hers, all passion unleashed. She felt his raging desire and instead of fear filling her, she rose on her toes and met his kiss with untamed passion. The letter fell as she slipped her hands over his shoulders and gripped him as he lifted her.

With a wildness she did not want to contain, Constance returned his kiss, trembling at the heat that coiled deep between her thighs. Their tongues tangled wildly, and she met him stroke for stroke, nip for nip. His kiss consumed her, need for him overwhelmed, and desire roared inside, beating in her veins like a fever. Her hands clasped and kneaded the muscled strength of his shoulders, then traveled to the dark luxuriance of his hair. She pulled the tie that held his hair in place, and thrust her fingers through his silky strands. She felt feverish and desperate.

His lips pulled from hers, and he trailed scalding kisses along her throat to the top of her exposed breasts. He tugged at laces of her dress, untying her corset with trembling fingers, revealing a thin chemisette. As he stared, her breasts got heavier and her nipples stabbed through the thin layers of her now soaked chemisette.

"Exquisite," he murmured softly, then dipped his head and sucked her through her clothes. Constance cried out, bucking sharply into his arms. Enflamed by his raw hunger, her body surged wantonly against him. His hands drew up the wet folds of her gown and his fingers unerringly found the slit in her drawers. He thrust two fingers deep inside of her and a moan broke low in her throat.

"You are so wet for me," he murmured around the nipple that he teased between his teeth.

She quaked, caught in a storm of passion. She was sinfully wet and she cared not if she was behaving scandalously.

He lifted his head. "Do you want me?"

A quiver of anticipation sliced through her. "Always,"

she promised.

"Night after night, you've haunted my dreams." He pressed a series of sensual little nips against her lips while they caught their breath. "I want to give you everything," he said, then he found her mouth again in a sweet, gentle kiss.

He withdrew from her and swung her fully into his arms and walked with her to the conservatory. She buried her face into his neck, hiding from the stinging rain until he slipped inside. Her heart clamored and deep excitement hummed inside of her. From the need thrumming from him she knew what would happen when they reached inside. She wanted it. She wanted him. The rain fell in earnest, but Constance was not cold. She burned, more from the desire coursing through her, than from the roaring fire in the hearth. Without speaking, she removed her soaked dress with his aid, petticoats and drawers, the silence drowning her with anticipation. When she stood before him naked, his gaze was a slow heated caress as it ran over her with possessive hunger.

He stepped back, stripped of his clothing, and she watched him with shameless desire. She had never seen an undressed man in all her years, and he was splendid. Powerful shoulders and chest adorned with black curls of hair formed a thin line from his sculptured chest, then arrowed down in a silken line over his hard, taut stomach. All that she had ever been curious about was bared to her gaze. Her mouth went dry at the large part of him that jutted toward her so boldly. She was enthralled with the sheer beauty of his body, its hardness and obvious strength. "You are beautiful, Lucan," she said on a gasp.

A pleased sensual smile curved his lips. "Do you know what I am going to do to you?"

"No." Though she had a fairly good idea from where he had touched and kissed her before.

"I am going to lay you on the chaise, and the first place I am going to kiss is between those thighs of yours. I have missed your sweet taste." His gaze moved possessively over her body. "I am going to splay your legs over my shoulders and unravel you as you ride my tongue."

Heat twisted her stomach in painful but exquisite knots. *Ride his tongue?* The imagery was enough to have dampness gathering between her thighs. A gentle breeze blew through the room, cooling the fire in her veins.

"And when you are ready for me," he gripped the hard, thick part of him that jutted out to her so proudly. "I am going to join us together."

Constance wasn't sure if she should be alarmed or intrigued. But before she could debate, he was there gathering her in his arms and laying her on the chaise and covering her like a warm sensual blanket. He then did exactly as he promised. He splayed her legs over his shoulders and kissed her *there*. His tongue dipped, licked, and caressed, both sensually teasing and passionately ravishing. He alternately sucked on her nub of pleasure until she thought she would expire from the exquisite torment, then flicked his tongue lower, devastating her with slow licks. She moaned helpless with pleasure, her body sensitized, shivering and trembling under the breath-taking assault of his erotic kiss against her core.

As if impatient for her, Lucan rose over her, lowering her legs to anchor at his hips. Acting on sheer instinct, she wrapped her legs high around the middle of his back and arched her hips. A blunt pressure pressed at her entrance, and he started to enter her. He sank deep and a startled moan of discomfort was wrenched from her. She stiffened at the bite of pain. Before she could question it he took her lips with tender ferocity. "Forgive me for the pain this will cause. It will be this one time, I promise." His lips claimed hers in a deeper kiss, and at the same time his hips flexed in a powerful move and he thrust into her fully.

The burning pain that jolted her, Constance had not expected. She bit into his lips deeply, until she tasted the coppery tang of blood. She pulled her lips from his and buried her face in his throat, shaking, trying to process the sensations racing through her. Pain blended with pleasure, and she did not know if she wanted him in her or away from her. Lucan held himself still, peppering kisses along her shoulder, murmuring crooning words. He lifted her face from the crook of his neck with a finger. His eyes searched her face intently and then a dark sensual smile curved his lips.

She could feel his heart beating against her breast. He brushed a soft kiss across her brow, the most fleeting of caress and her heart clenched. Her eyes widened as he slowly pulled from her and sank back in her heat with shocking strength, encouraging her tender flesh to yield to his possession. The feel of him inside her, stretching her, filling her, was the most glorious sensation Constance had ever felt. He moved with long powerful strokes, and she gasped in sudden delight at the sensation that raced through her.

He lowered his head to capture an achingly sensitive nipple as he thrust deeper and harder. Ripples of pleasure began to build in Constance and broken moans were wrenched from her as exquisite pleasure-pain coiled and build inside.

There was pleasure and pain, sweetness and delight, but Constance yearned for something *more*. "Lucan," her cry of his name was needy, desperate.

He released her nipple and claimed her lips in a scorching kiss. It was more than a kiss; he made love to her mouth as he worshipped her body with his. It was sweet, wild, and more intense than anything she had ever felt. "You are so beautiful in your passion," he groaned. He kissed her hair, whispering praises and love, as if he couldn't stop.

Her hands slicked over his sweat dampened skin as she held onto him while he rode her with deeper strokes. Delight pulsed in Constance, thrummed and expanded until nothing but heat and need filled her, then exploded into pleasure so hot and destructive she screamed. He brought her to the same pinnacle at least three more times until with a deep groan he fell with her.

• • •

Lucan was painfully aware Constance had not spoken words of love. Though he knew she had to feel something for him or she would never have gifted him her body, some doubt snaked in. He knew full well passion and love were two separate entities. The words themselves were trapped in his heart, yearning to spill free, but something locked them inside of him. It was as if he needed to hear her declaration. She lay on her stomach, soft, pliant, purring in her throat in completion. He kissed her shoulder blades and peppered soft kisses along her spine with gentle nips down to her buttocks. He had missed her so damn much. Her taste, her scent, her laughter. The fierce love making they had just tumbled in would not be enough to sate the raw need he felt for her. He doubted any amount of loving would satiate him.

The lush curves of her hips and her buttocks enticed, and he kept up a soft nibble and lick of her skin down to the curve of her hips. Her soft sighs and shivers had lust coiling in his gut and he wanted her on her knees, on his cock. He restrained the need, struggling to remember that despite her lush sensuality Constance was an innocent. Then she rolled her hips in invitation, and he groaned low in his throat. He had just spent deep inside of her, but he hardened again in a fierce rush of desire.

He came down on his elbow over her, and she turned her head to meet his lips in a kiss that shocked him with its raw carnality. Want slammed into him, hot and hungry and his hand tightened on her hips. She moaned into the kiss, her tongue stroking his in ravenous delight, her hips arching and rolling underneath him, teasing him, tempting him to lose control.

Breaking the kiss, he drew her roughly onto her knees. Instead of keeping her there, he sat back on his haunches and drew her up so that she straddled his thighs, the soft of her back pressing into his chest. Using his thighs, Lucan nudge her wider and notched the head of his cock at her slick entrance.

"*Hmmm*," she all but purred, arching into him as he cupped her breasts from behind, rolling her nipples between his fingers. "I like this, Lucan," she said on a throaty sigh, then a soft chuckle filled with delight echoed from her.

"I live to please you," he teased, placing a soft kiss on her shoulder. Unable to wait, Lucan slid his hand from her breast to her hip to hold her steady and plunged inside her tight wetness in a deep surge. Her cry and his groan entwined in the conservatory, and though rain fell in earnest outside, sweat slicked both their skins. With another two hard thrusts, he buried himself fully inside her, then held still so she could adjust to the thickness of him. Lucan was aware of how large he must feel to her, because she was so damn snug she strangled his cock.

"Ride me," he growled, shocking himself with the harsh command. *Damn.* He struggled to remember her innocence, but before he could take back the order, Constance's hips rolled, slow, sinuous, stroking him with her tight clasp, sending a cascading wave of shiver down his spine. The latent sensuality in the movement surprised and enthralled him. Her hips arched as she slid up so the tip of his cock was at her entrance, then lowered onto him with exquisite slowness. She sank down on his thick length, biting her lip, her face a study of deep determination and lust. She whimpered and curled her hands behind his neck, the move thrusting her breast further out in a perfect arch, and tilted her face to his. "Like this?" she asked with a soft moan as she glided up his length and down again.

"Yes," the words hissed from his teeth as she tightened and rippled over his cock, shooting hot prickling sensation to his balls.

The amusement in her green eyes, along with the hunger beguiled him. "I do like to ride," she drawled her voice husky with laughter and desire. Then she proceeded to take him with a ride that was pure torture. His stomach walls tightened as he fought the need to take control. She was moving so damn slow, so beautifully slow, taking him to the edge of pleasure and keeping him there. What he loved the most about her movements was how natural, sweet and powerful they were.

Nothing practiced, only the innate sensuality she had always shimmered with.

He snaked his hand from her hip and delved between her curls finding her clitoris and caressing her with a slow flick. She jerked and shivered in his embrace, and he placed a wet kiss on her neck. She tightened on his cock further and the guttural groan that she pulled from his throat rumbled in the room. Fisting her mane of hair in his hand, he tilted her head more and took her lips in a wet kiss. Hunger burned away the doubts and the fear, and he sank with her until he lowered her to her elbows, her hips nestled into his. He released her lips and met her aroused gaze. The emotions that glittered in her emerald eyes humbled him.

"Lucan, I love you so much it hurts," she declared with raw sincerity.

It was as if her words shattered the tenuous control he had, and he withdrew and slammed into her tight core with bruising force. But she took him, rolled her hips back on him, taking his passion, meeting him thrust for thrust. A needy moan hissed from her lips and traveled straight to his balls tightening them, making him more insatiable in his rough demands. Her hips jerked in time to his hard, deep thrust as he sank into her over and over, and her cries of love wrapped around his soul. "I love you, Constance," he breathed fiercely as pleasure overwhelmed him. His fingers dug into the lush curve of her hips as he plunged and retreated into her convulsing body, riding them both into one orgasm after the other.

• • •

Constance lay in Lucan's arms with the aftershocks of pleasure coursing through her. Never could she have imagined this delight in being intimate. She liked it. A soft laugh puffed from her. She more than liked it. She laced her fingers through Lucan's own and shifted so that she lay more comfortably in the crook of his arms.

"We could marry here in the village or in London if you wish. Lady Calydon would host our engagement announcement at Sherring Cross, and then we could marry a few weeks later. The Archbishop of Canterbury would conduct our wedding. I have instructed a nursery to have two thousand white roses for any day you so desire. The orchestra from the royal academy of music will play for you as you walk down the aisle," Lucan said.

She tilted her chin to stare at him. Joy bubbled inside of her. "My dream wedding," she mused softly. "Only Sebastian and Anthony knew exactly what I wanted."

"Calydon told me," he admitted gruffly.

"That's interesting," she murmured, gliding her fingertips over their laced knuckles. "But I do not want all that."

"Constance, I—"

She rolled onto him, drawing her knees up to bracket his hips as she sat on him fully. An arrested expression crossed his face. "I do not care for the dreams I had before. I do not wish for a grand ceremony, or even a dress by Worth in Paris anymore. I yearn to be your wife, your duchess, your light, the joy and solace in your life, Lucan. That is what I want."

A slow breath exhaled from him and a smile of tenderness creased his lips. "I do have a special license in my desk."

She blinked down at him and then a light laugh pulsed from her, joy suffusing her heart. "Hopeful weren't you?"

"More than you can ever know," he said pulling her

head down to claim her lips tenderly.

Hours passed in the conservatory as Lucan introduced her to blissful pleasure. They laughed, they talked and they made love some more. Nothing mattered to Constance other than knowing she was in the arms of the man who cherished her more than anything in his world.

Epilogue

ONE WEEK LATER

Early morning sunlight streamed into the bedchamber and splashed across the sheets. Constance lay curved on her side, a wealth of rich golden hair spilled down her shoulders to her back. Her head was pillowed on Lucan's arm, and she breathed softly and evenly. She was a warm comforting weight on his chest, and he loved her. *She is so perfect*, he thought, awed. Her passion, her generosity in wedding him, despite the monstrous way he had treated her, her kindness.

They had married only three days after she had visited him at Wynter Park to the chagrin of her mother, Lady Radcliffe. Constance had been firm in her decision, ignoring cajoling from Lady Calydon and Lady Phillipa for a grand wedding. Lucan and Constance had married in a small intimate ceremony with only family members at the chapel at Wynter Park.

After a small wedding breakfast, everyone had departed, and he had swept a giggling Constance off her feet to their chamber. The past few days had been a blur of a sensual feast and unending delight as they learned each other. She exemplified passion, in everything she did, and Lucan's heart still lurched from time to time when he thought of how he could have lost her.

Wedding gifts and wishes had come pouring in, with an expediency that startled them. They were, after all, in Suffolk. The best one, that had placed a very satisfied smile on his sweet wife's face, was the package sent by Lord Ainsley. A clipping from *The Spectator*. It had read:

> *Lady X has learned the most delightful news and is eager to share with like-minded admirers of the beautiful Lady Constance, the Untouchable One. Much to the dismay of many maters of society, she is now the Duchess of Mondvale, having married yesterday in a quiet ceremony, which has not been announced in any official papers as yet. A close family friend revealed it is indeed a love match, as the gracious and charming Lady Mondvale only consented to marry the Lord of Sin after leading him on a well-deserved merry chase. Congratulations to our most famous newlyweds of the season. May your life be filled with joy, happiness, and scandalous delights. We raise our glasses to Duke and Duchess Mondvale.*

Acknowledgments

I thank God every day for allowing me to find my passion.

To my husband, whom I adore. Thank you for being my biggest fan and supporter, and for loving the fact that I am a ninja in disguise. Also for reading all my drafts and listening to me plot ideas at three a.m.! You are so damn amazing.

Thank you to my wonderful editors, Nina Bruhns and Alycia Tornetta for shaping Sins of a Duke into a gem.

Many thanks to Robyn DeHart for allowing her wonderful character Lady Vivian Ashford, The Paragon, who has captured the heart of many readers in her book A Little Bit Wicked to grace the pages of Sins of a Duke.

To historical romance author Giselle Marks and Frances Fowlkes for being fabulous critique partners.

To my wonderful readers, thank you for picking up my book and giving me a chance! You guys rock! Special shout out to my Rioters. Just hanging with you guys, talking books, Walking Dead, and Banshee keeps me sane! Thank you.

Special THANK YOU to everyone that leaves a review, bloggers, fans, friends....I have always said reviews to authors are like a pot of gold to Leprechauns. Thank you all for adding to my rainbow one review at a time.

About the Author

Stacy Reid is an avid reader of novels with a deep passion for writing. She especially loves romance and enjoys writing about people falling in love. She lives a lot in the worlds she creates and she actively speaks to her characters (out loud). She has a warrior way "Never give up on my dream." When she is not writing, she spends a copious amount of time drooling over Rick Grimes from Walking Dead, Lucas Hood from Banshee, watching Japanese Anime and playing video games with her love — Dusean. She also has a horrible weakness for Ice cream.

She is always happy to hear from readers and would love for you to connect with her via Website | Facebook | Twitter

To be the first to hear about her new releases, get cover reveals and excerpts you won't find anywhere else, sign up for her Newsletter, or join her in The Riot.

Happy reading!

Made in the USA
San Bernardino, CA
23 July 2016